# THE

# $\mathcal{S}$OLICITOR'S

# SON

# THE
# $\mathscr{S}$OLICITOR'S
# SON

# RACHAEL
# ANDERSON

HEA Publishing

Cover image credit: Ilina Simeonova/Trevillion images

ISBN: 978-1-941363-26-3

Published by HEA Publishing

FOR MY AWESOME READERS

THANK YOU

OTHER BOOKS BY RACHAEL ANDERSON

**Regency Novels**
*My Sister's Intended* (Serendipity 1)
*My Brother's Bride* (Serendipity 2)
*The Fall of Lord Drayson* (Tanglewood 1)
*The Rise of Miss Notley* (Tanglewood 2)
*The Pursuit of Lady Harriett* (Tanglewood 3)

**Contemporary Novels**
*Prejudice Meets Pride* (Meet Your Match 1)
*Rough Around the Edges Meets Refined* (Meet Your Match 2)
*Stick in the Mud Meets Spontaneity* (Meet Your Match 3)
*Not Always Happenstance* (Power of the Matchmaker)
*The Reluctant Bachelorette*
*Working it Out*
*Minor Adjustments*
*Luck of the Draw*
*Divinely Designed*

**Novellas**
*Righting a Wrong*
*Twist of Fate*
*The Meltdown Match*

# ONE

HUGH QUINTON SCOWLED at the numbers scribbled on the ledger before him. Another two hundred pounds to the tailor? Good gads. How many clothes did Lord Lister own? Perhaps he was in the habit of wearing a shirt once and tossing it out. If so, the man was a fool, and Hugh didn't do business with fools.

He snapped the ledger closed and sat back on the chair in his study. One frivolous purchase after another. A Grecian urn for the remains of Lady Lister's deceased cat. Trained parrots for their daughter's comeout ball, imported lace for draperies, and Hugh could scarcely believe the sum that had been paid to a traveling gypsy for an elixir that purportedly healed any ailment—with the exception of stupidity, apparently.

Hugh had been assured that Lord Lister's estate was in dire need of help, but in truth, the only help the man needed was for someone to take away his pocketbook and his ability to purchase on credit.

The door opened a crack, and the one servant Hugh employed popped his head through the opening. Tall and gangly, with cropped red hair, overly long arms, and freckles, Park had the appearance of an underfed monkey. How he could be underfed, Hugh had no idea. The man ate enough for three grown men.

"The Viscount Knave's 'ere to see you." Park twirled what Hugh assumed was a calling card through his fingers the way a magician might. Only instead of making it disappear, he flicked it in the air and deftly caught it with his opposite hand. The man was an expert at card tricks and couldn't hand over a calling card without a performance.

Hugh's brow puckered. "Do I know the Viscount Knave?" The name didn't sound familiar.

"'Ow should I know? I don't keep a log of every toff you meet." Two years ago, Edwin Parker appeared on Hugh's doorstep to answer his ad for a manservant. The gangly fellow had been as cheeky then as he was now, insisting to be called only Park. Apparently, Edwin made him sound like a stiff, and a stiff he was not.

"Park'll do me just fine," he'd told Hugh, his gaze direct and unwavering.

Hugh, an admirer of spunk, hired him on the spot. It had been the right decision. Although Park could be a bit too bold at times, he was shrewd, clever, loyal, and someone Hugh had grown to respect. He was also a decent cook when he set his mind to it. He'd even taught Hugh how to make beefsteak.

Hugh slid the ledger to Park. "You may show Lord Knave in and return this to Lord Lister. Tell him that the only recommendation I have is to cut his spending by at least fifty percent. His land steward has his estate well in hand already. There is nothing more I can do."

Park grinned as he swapped the calling card for the ledger. "Always 'appy to tell a bloke what's what." He loved imparting news of this nature—the kind that put "toffs" in their place, as Park referred to them. He wasn't one to soften words, preferring to deliver them with his signature audacity. In this instance, Hugh would let him.

As soon as Park had gone, Hugh picked up the calling card and studied the name. *Lord Knave, Lord Knave, Lord Knave.* He couldn't remember meeting anyone by that name. Perhaps he was a friend of a former client who had heard Hugh's name bandied about in conversation. As word of Hugh's abilities continued to spread, it was not uncommon for a stranger to contact him.

"Last door on the left, milord," came Park's voice from down the hall. "No, not that 'un. The *last* door."

Hugh rolled his eyes. He'd told Park time and time again that he should show their guests all the way to the study, but the man could rarely be bothered. One of these days, Hugh should threaten to sack him if he didn't comply, not that it would do much good. Park knew he never would.

A tall, dark-haired man stepped into the room and gave Hugh a quick appraisal. Hugh did the same. Dressed well but not extravagantly so, Lord Knave had an intelligent look about him. He carried himself with confidence—not pride or condescension, as many men of his station did—just . . . confidence. Hugh respected that.

He stood and extended a hand. "Lord Knave, I presume? I'm Hugh Quinton."

"I assumed as much," he said.

They shook hands, and Hugh gestured to the chair on the other side of his large desk. "Please, have a seat."

Lord Knave settled down and glanced around the room, no doubt noticing the shabby furnishings. Hugh didn't mind. The desk, armchairs, and bookcases were well worn, but they were sturdy and had served him well over the past few years. Unlike Lord Lister, Hugh didn't spend money that didn't need to be spent.

"You have an interesting butler, Mr. Quinton," said Lord Knave.

Hugh leaned his elbows on the desk and interlocked his fingers. "I wouldn't call Park a butler."

"What would you call him?"

"A stray—or rather, a scalawag I've hired to help with various duties, answering doors the least among them."

Lord Knave nodded in understanding. "I have a friend who likes to harbor strays as well. Only in her case, they're animals."

"Animals probably make less noise and are better behaved than Park," said Hugh wryly. "What can I do for you, my lord?"

He leaned back in his chair and pressed his lips together a moment before speaking. "I've come to invite you to a summer house party at my family's estate in Oxfordshire the beginning of August." He spoke as though it were an every-day occurrence to invite a tradesman to an upper class party, and a stranger at that.

Hugh furrowed his brow. "A summer house party, you say?"

"Yes."

"Forgive me, my lord, but you don't know me, and we certainly don't run in the same circles. What possible reason could you have to issue such an invitation?"

"I have a task for you."

*Ah, there's the rub.* "What sort of task?"

"You have earned a reputation as a polished and shrewd businessman. I would like you to come to the party as my guest, and while there, evaluate the dealings of the neighboring estate—discreetly, of course. It is owned by my father-in-law who isn't, let us say, *as* shrewd. Despite his best efforts, he is running his property into the ground, and I can no longer stand by and watch him bring ruin upon himself and his family. I am hopeful that you will be of some help in that quarter."

Hugh could already think of several problems with this plan, including the fact that he never committed himself to anything without prior knowledge of the owner or estate. His reputation stemmed from his many successes, and he wasn't about to jeopardize that by agreeing to help a man who, like Lord Lister, wasn't in a place to be helped.

"To do a full analysis, I would need access to his ledgers and all business dealings over the past several years. I would need to speak with his steward, housekeeper, butler, and even his tenants. I don't see how any of that would be possible if I stay as a guest in another man's house."

"My wife and I shall see that you have access to anything you need," said Lord Knave.

Hugh wasn't even close to being convinced. "I make a habit of looking at the ledgers *before* I decide if my services will be of value."

Lord Knave didn't respond right away. He brushed something—a bit of lint, perhaps?—from his pantaloons before looking up. "I can't provide you with the ledgers at this time, but I'd be happy to answer any questions you have about the estate. I've become very familiar with it over the past few years."

Hugh leaned back in his chair and folded his arms. "I assume you have your own property well in hand?"

"Yes."

"Is there a reason *you* haven't come to his aid?"

"I have already done what I can. When Lady Knave and I married, my family agreed to pay off her father's debts in exchange for some unused land he owned. I'd hoped that would be enough to set him on a more lucrative course, but in recent years, he's agreed to sell off parcels of farmland to some of his tenants. Although the funds padded his purse for a time, his rents are now down, and he has been forced to use those funds to keep himself afloat. If things continue as they are, he'll be back in debt in another year."

Hugh was even less convinced than before, if possible. Although Lord Knave obviously had his father-in-law's best interests at heart, compassion could only go so far in matters of business. Good sense was far more important, and it didn't sound as though the gentleman in question possessed much of that.

"What would you like me to do, exactly?" Hugh had aided the proprietors of many estates, but he was no miracle worker. He couldn't summon money from nothing. "If his rents no longer cover his expenditures, I don't see how I can possibly be of service, other than to suggest that he economize as much as possible."

Lord Knave nodded slowly, but the determination in his expression told Hugh he wasn't ready to capitulate. "Whether or not you can help remains to be seen. I would like you to accompany me to Lynfield and observe the state of things for yourself. You will be more than compensated for your troubles. Come, Mr. Quinton, say you will join our little house party and give me your opinion on Talford Hall."

At his words, Hugh's entire body tensed. *Lynfield. Talford Hall.* Now *those* were names he knew all too well. Charming countryside. Gray stone walls covered in ivy, large windows overlooking lush grounds, and four tall chimney stacks that towered above the roofline, looking like watch towers—at least that's what he'd imagined them to be as a lad.

"Who is your father-in-law?" Hugh kept his tone neutral, but the moment Lord Knave said, "Mr. John

Gifford," Hugh's jaw clenched and his fingers tightened around the arms of his chair. Another name Hugh knew well. He could still imagine the cold, hard gleam in the man's eyes.

As a boy of not yet fourteen, Hugh had once accompanied his newly-widowed father almost daily to Talford Hall. While his father worked to organize Mr. Gifford's affairs and strategize possible investment opportunities, Hugh was left to twiddle his thumbs in the kitchen or gardens.

It would have been miserable in the extreme had he not encountered the eldest Gifford daughter that first afternoon. Only a few years his junior, Sophie's quick wit and kind spirit endeared her to him instantly. They'd become fast friends, and on the afternoons Hugh came to visit, she grew adept at evading her governess.

As the weeks passed, they enjoyed many adventures, and Hugh always made a point of returning to the kitchen before his father's expected departure. Even at their tender ages, he and Sophie had both known it wasn't seemly for a gentleman's daughter and a solicitor's son to form any sort of attachment, even friendship.

One rainy afternoon, late that summer, Sophie lost her boot in the muddy banks of a stream. They searched for a long while, and when it couldn't be found, Hugh gallantly offered to carry her from the woods. It was at that inopportune time they were discovered by Hugh's father and Mr. Gifford.

Both children were coated in mud, soaked to the bone, and laughing hysterically. Mr. Gifford had taken one look at his daughter's exposed foot before he snatched Sophie from Hugh's hold. Without asking for an explanation, he dismissed Hugh's father on the spot and sent them both away.

Not only had he refused to pay Hugh's father for the services rendered, but shortly thereafter, word spread that Mr. Jacob Quinton, solicitor and advisor to several in the area, could no longer be trusted. By the culmination of that year, Hugh's father was forced to seek a living elsewhere.

Those had been dark and difficult times—times Hugh would likely never forget *or* forgive.

He pushed his chair back and stood. "I'm sorry you have come for naught, my lord, but I cannot help you. If you'll follow me, I'll show you to the door."

Lord Knave looked momentarily surprised, then slowly nodded as if he understood. "No need. I can show myself out."

Lord Knave's steps were slow as he moved towards the door. With one hand on the knob, he paused to look back at Hugh. "I should tell you that my father-in-law isn't the only one who will suffer should the estate fall to ruin. My sister-in-law, Miss Sophia Gifford, stands to inherit."

Hugh looked sharply at Lord Knave. There was a knowing look in his expression, as though he was aware of the history between the Quintons and Giffords. Had Sophie told him? Was *she* the reason Lord Knave stood before Hugh now?

The thought had a softening effect on his anger. He could never be angry with Sophie.

Hugh had begun that summer in a dark and lonely place, having just lost his mother. He hadn't wanted to go with his father to Talford Hall. He hadn't wanted to go anywhere. But the moment he'd met Sophie, everything changed. Her smile made him smile, her quick wit reminded him how to laugh, and her love of animals had touched his heart. She'd brightened his world, showed him there was still much joy to be found, and became his dearest friend. He could never turn his back on her.

Her father, on the other hand, deserved nothing but contempt.

A pain pierced his forehead, and Hugh pinched the bridge of his nose with his fingers. Could he bring himself to help her father?

*You wouldn't be helping* him. *You'd be helping* her.

Hugh dropped his hand to his side and exhaled a frustrated sigh. He half glared at the man who'd just made it impossible to say no.

Lord Knave pulled a folded missive from inside his coat pocket and tossed it on his desk. "An invitation to the house party should you change your mind. Good day to you."

Hugh watched him leave before he dropped to his chair and rested his forehead against the palms of his hand. He stared at his name written across the invitation in an elegant, feminine script. Had Sophie written that? Did she know her brother-in-law had come seeking Hugh's help? Did she even remember her childhood friend?

With a sigh, he pulled open the bottom desk drawer and fingered past several files until he came to one marked *Personal*. Although he'd never call himself sentimental, there were a handful of letters he'd never been able to part with. A note written by his mother before her death, a letter his father had sent him after he'd gone away to school for the first time, and . . . Sophie's.

He lifted the tattered, faded page and read the words he hadn't read in years. This letter had once carried him through the time when he and his father had been forced to leave the house they'd always called home and begin anew.

*Dearest Hugh,*

*I had to sneak into my father's study last night to learn your direction. I can only hope you are still in* residence. *In truth, I'm unsure how I will post this letter, but I will find a way.*

*I am so angry with Papa for what he has done. He has taken my friend from me in the most abominable manner, and I cannot forgive him or the cruel way he dismissed your father. I tried to explain, but he wouldn't listen. I feel as though it's my fault for getting stuck in that horrid mud and losing my boot. I'm so dreadfully sorry.*

*I know we cannot exchange letters because it will only anger Papa more, but I had to let you know that I will always think of you as my dearest friend. You have taught me how to fish and swim. You have helped me ride with more confidence and climb trees. Because of you, I'm no longer afraid to catch grass-hoppers and frogs, but I will continue to draw the line at snakes—they will always be vile, untrustworthy creatures.*

*You, on the other hand, are not the least bit vile or untrustworthy. You are the best kind of person. Don't ever change, and don't stop thinking of me as your friend. I know I won't.*

*Someday, if we are both very good, perhaps we shall meet again. I will hope for it with all my heart.*

*Sophie*

Hugh dropped the letter on his desk and swiveled the top half of his wooden chair around to face the lone window in his study. His small London townhome was situated on the outskirts of Lambeth, not far from Vauxhall Gardens. The surrounding streets housed a great many artisans, clerks, and other tradesmen. Even with the interminable fog hovering about, Hugh felt comfortable here. This was where he belonged, not on the other side of the Thames near Mayfair or St. James's or even Upper Seymour Street, and certainly not at a summer house party at the home of Lord and Lady Knave.

Blast his wretched conscience.

# TWO

THE DOOR TO Sophia Gifford's bedchamber flew open, and through the looking glass above her dressing table, she saw a flurry of purple taffeta enter the room in the form of her mother. Oh, what a sight. Her mother's golden ringlets were only half pinned back, making her appear a bit like a poodle that had only been partially trimmed. Apparently, she'd thought it more imperative to speak to her daughter than complete her toilette.

"I hear you are engaged to drive with Mr. Fawcett again," her mother said in a displeased tone.

Sophia pulled on her gloves, examined her reflection one last time, and checked to make sure her blue velour bonnet was still in place. This particular shade, somewhat dusty in nature, served to temper the red in her hair and make her eyes appear more blue than hazel. It would do nicely for an outing in Hyde Park.

She looked back at her mother's reflection and nodded. "I am."

Sophia could almost see the steam exit her mother's nostrils. "Why do you keep encouraging that man?"

"Mr. Fawcett is congenial and kind. I enjoy his company." Sophia pinched her cheeks to give them some color and stood.

13

"He is not titled, and his income is paltry at best."

Sophia was well aware of those facts. She was also aware that her third London season was nearing its end, and Mr. Fawcett was the only suitor she'd ever been able to contemplate marrying. With her younger sister, Prudence, already married, Sophia was firmly on the shelf. If Mr. Fawcett failed to come up to scratch, Sophia feared she would live the remainder of her life husbandless.

"I don't care about that," said Sophia. If nothing else, the past three years had taught her to speak her mind more forcefully. How timid she used to be.

"But Lord Daglum will be calling shortly. I told him only last evening that you would be at home this morning."

That was precisely why Sophia had sent a note to Mr. Fawcett earlier, asking if he would consider moving up the time of their drive. His response had come quickly.

*With the greatest pleasure.*
*—Mr. Fawcett*

Yes, most congenial.

Sophia reached for her pelisse. "You will be here to receive Lord Daglum, will you not, Mother? I'm certain he would prefer to speak with you anyway. You are infinitely more diverting than me."

Not surprisingly, her flattery fell on deaf ears. "He's not coming to speak with me. He is coming to speak with *you*."

"No. He is coming to pander and flatter for the sole purpose of getting his hands on my dowry. It is a well-known fact that his pockets are to let. He doesn't care a groat about me."

"That is not true. Only last evening, he mentioned how kind and elegant you are, and he very much wished you had accompanied me to the musicale. He is also titled, and his connections are far superior to those of Mr. Fawcett's."

Sophia rolled her eyes. "Lord Daglum cares for three things at present: his beloved Arabian, my inheritance, and his mistress. In that order."

Her mother gasped. "You should not speak of such things, let alone know about them."

"Well I do," said Sophia, "and I'd as lief live alone than with a man who places greater value on his horse than his wife."

Her mother's eyebrows narrowed into a glare. "This is your sister's doing, isn't it? Those ridiculous stories she writes have corrupted you into thinking that—"

As if on cue, Prudence came rushing into the room, her lovely dark curls bouncing at the sides of her flushed cheeks.

She greeted their mother quickly before grasping her sister's hands. "Soph, I have the most wonderful news. Knave and I are to throw a house party this summer. Say you will help me organize it. I shall need you throughout the entire process if it is to be successful, and I so badly want it to be a success."

"I don't see how that will be possible," said their mother dryly. "Sophia will be planning her wedding and won't have time for summer house parties."

Sophia rolled her eyes. Her mother knew full well that Prudence didn't want Sophia marrying Mr. Fawcett any more than their mother did, only for different reasons.

Sure enough, Prudence's smile vanished. "Has Mr. Fawcett made you on offer? Do not say you have agreed!"

Sophia threw up her hands, ready to be done with this conversation. "No, he has not made me an offer."

"Then why this nonsense about wedding plans?"

"Should he make her an offer," said their unhelpful

mother, "she has every intention of accepting him, not that your father would give his consent."

"I am of age, Mother. I do not need his consent."

That had been the wrong thing to say because two sets of eyes grew very wide. Prudence was the first to speak. "How can you consider marrying a man you do not love?"

"Oh, for pity's sake," said their mother. "Stop filling her head with such nonsense. Sophia would have married Lord Ponsonby during her first season had you not dissuaded her with talk of love."

"Do give me some credit, Mother. Lord Ponsonby was old enough to be my father. Prudence had nothing to do with my dismissal of his suit."

"Marrying for love is not nonsense," added Prudence, her dark eyes flashing with conviction. "Every woman should seek for such a union, especially Sophia. She's more deserving than anyone."

Their mother looked sharply at Prudence. "You were fortunate enough to fall in love with a man who is titled, wealthy, and well-connected, although you certainly strained those connections when you insisted on publishing that . . . that story."

"It is called a romance novel, and I intend to publish more. Perhaps then more women would favor love in lieu of connections."

"Unfortunately, your sister favors neither. Or have you forgotten she intends to wed a man she does not love and who is not well connected. She would be better off marrying Lord Daglum."

"Lord *Brag*lum, you mean," Prudence muttered.

"I beg your pardon?" said their mother.

"Sophia would be miserable the rest of her life," said Prudence more firmly. "I would never allow that to happen."

They continued to argue, and Sophia had to close her eyes and breathe deeply to keep from shouting at them to stop. Her mother and sister seemed to think they knew what was best, but Sophia couldn't take their matchmaking any longer. It was time to move on with her life and be done with this once and for all.

"Mother," Sophia finally blurted. "Lord Daglum will be calling shortly, and your hair is only half pinned. Shouldn't you—"

"Merciful heavens!" Her hands flew to her head. One glance in Sophia's looking glass sent her rushing from the room, purple taffeta rustling once more.

Sophia felt a small measure of relief, but when her gaze landed on her younger sister, she grew wary. "I will be glad to help you plan your summer party at a later time, Pru. This morning, I am engaged to drive with Mr. Fawcett."

Prudence plopped down on Sophia's bed, her expression determined. "You will not be rid of me as easily as Mother."

Sophia had assumed as much and sighed inwardly. Prudence had always been stubborn.

"You are not seriously considering wedding Mr. Fawcett, are you?" she asked.

"I am twenty-two, Pru," Sophia said. "He is kind, congenial, and I believe he genuinely cares for me. What more can I hope for in a match?"

"Oh, I don't know." Prudence's voice dripped with sarcasm. "Love, perhaps? Happiness? Bliss?"

"I said what more could *I* hope for." Sophia's tone was more wry than sad. Long ago, she'd accepted the fact that her life would be different than her sister's. "I am not you, and I could never hope to be you. For me, Mr. Fawcett is enough."

"You speak of him as though he is merely a friend."

"He *is* a friend. A very dear friend."

"That is no basis for a marriage."

"I disagree. I think it a very good basis. Can you not count Knave among your very dear friends?"

"Of course," said Prudence, her brow crinkled in worry. "I didn't mean it that way. I agree that friendship is paramount, but . . . I just wish for you to have more than that in your marriage. I want you to have what I have with Knave."

Sophia smiled sadly. Deep down, she yearned for the same, but after three years of searching The Marriage Mart in vain, she'd finally come to the realization that if she didn't settle for something less than love, she'd live the remainder of her life trapped with her parents and treated like a child.

"Tell me this, Pru," said Sophia. "Is it better to marry a dear friend or remain as I am?"

Prudence opened her mouth to argue, but she seemed to realize she had no argument to make and pressed her lips together instead. After a moment, she asked, "You're determined?"

"I'm determined."

"Will you at least delay your acceptance until after my house party?"

Sophia nearly laughed. "Honestly, Pru. You're perfectly capable of planning a party on your own. You don't need me."

"Oh, but I do—well, not *need* you, per se. But two minds are preferable to one, are they not? It will be much more fun to scheme with you."

Sophia couldn't help but smile at that. Prudence had always made her feel needed, and she adored her sister for that. But if Mr. Fawcett did indeed come up to scratch, how could she possibly waylay him? It didn't seem fair or even reasonable to ask such a thing.

"I can suggest that we marry later in the fall. That way, all wedding plans can wait until after your house party."

"Oh, that will not do at all. You'd be betrothed!"

"That *is* what happens when one accepts a marriage proposal," Sophia said dryly. "Is that a problem?"

"Yes."

"I can't imagine why."

"Because . . ." Prudence blustered a moment before adding, "Because that would leave Catherine as the only unattached woman at our party, and how dreadfully awkward for her."

"Perhaps you should expand your invitation list," Sophia suggested.

"And perhaps you should wait until after the party to become betrothed to Mr. Fawcett. I hardly know the man, after all. Can you not give me a little time to further our acquaintance before you commit yourself to him?"

Sophia raised an eyebrow. "You've had plenty of opportunities to 'further your acquaintance' as you say, but you haven't chosen to do so."

"I didn't realize you were seriously considering him."

"I am."

Prudence nodded slowly, and she seemed to force her next words out. "Well, now that I know you are in earnest, I will do my best to . . ."

"Further your acquaintance?"

"Er . . . yes." Prudence pressed her lips together again, only this time in consternation. After a moment, her brow cleared, and she looked her sister in the eye. With her usual frankness, she asked, "Do you truly wish to wed Mr. Fawcett? If you can honestly answer yes, I will not stand in your way. But if you cannot, then I beg of you, give it a little more time—at least until the end of August."

Sophia opened her mouth to say that she *did* wish to marry him, but her conscience wouldn't allow her to speak words she did not know to be true. Mr. Fawcett was a good man. He was also easy to converse with and valued her opinions. He didn't care that she adored animals or had freckles, and he made her laugh on occasion. He was exactly the sort of man she *should* want to marry.

The trouble was, when he kissed her hand, she felt nothing. When they sat close enough that their shoulders brushed, she didn't yearn for more. And when he smiled at her, her stomach didn't twirl or do any of that nonsense Prudence wrote about in her books. Though it didn't really sound like nonsense to Sophia. It sounded wonderful.

"I'll take that as my answer," said Prudence with a pointed look. "Don't marry him, Soph. He's not right for you."

"What if no man is right for me?" Sophia asked quietly, finally voicing her greatest fear. "I want more than animals to care for, Pru. I want a husband and children of my own."

"And you shall have all of that," said Prudence in earnest. "You need only be a little more patient."

Sophia shook her head, having lost faith in patience long ago. "I've given it three seasons already. I'm on the shelf with fewer and fewer prospects each year. In all this time, Mr. Fawcett is the only man who has shown a genuine interest in me that I also happen to like. I would be a fool to dismiss him."

Prudence opened her mouth to argue, but Sophia wasn't finished. She raised a hand and continued, "That said, if you invite Mr. Fawcett to your house party, perhaps he will not feel the need to offer for me before the season's end. That will give us both a little more time."

The compromise didn't seem to appease her sister, but

after a moment, Prudence finally nodded. "I suppose if I am to get to know him, you must invite him. But I don't have to like it."

Sophia's chuckle was interrupted by a maid at the door. "Mr. Fawcett's 'ere to see you, Miss," she said, bobbing a quick curtsy.

"Thank you." Sophia collected her shawl and reticule, then paused at the door to glance back at her sister. "Give him a chance, Pru. Perhaps he will surprise us both."

# THREE

**Six Weeks Later**

SOPHIA PAUSED AT the bottom of the stairs in her sister's home. While it was good to be back in the village of Lynfield, Oxfordshire, the place she'd always felt most at peace, a curious uneasiness assaulted her, along with the sound of voices coming from the drawing room. Mr. Fawcett arrived earlier that afternoon, and although the house party wouldn't officially begin until the morrow—when the last of their friends were to arrive—the burden of expectations hung heavy in the air.

She glanced around the great hall of Radbourne Abbey, home to Knave's parents, Lord and Lady Bradden. Quaintly situated next to her own family's estate, Sophia had always admired its Palladian architecture. But as she examined the opulence surrounding her, she felt as she often had during her past three seasons—out of place. She preferred her family's more modest seat of Talford Hall, with its well-worn furniture, squeaky fourth stair, and her bedchamber window that overlooked the stables.

She would have stayed there for the duration of the house party, had it not been for her sister's insistence that she remain at Radbourne—and the fact that her parents would be at Talford. At least here she could distance herself from her mother's constant hen-pecking and ride Dominicus whenever she pleased.

Oh, how she loved to ride.

She was sorely tempted to sneak away to the stables now and avoid dinner altogether, but Prudence would never forgive her.

Sophia smoothed her hands down the front of her sea-green gown—the one her sister had insisted she wear—and took a deep breath. Honestly, why was she so nervous? Aside from Prudence's in-laws and her family, only Mr. Fawcett would be in attendance tonight. She should save her nerves for the morrow, when the dreaded Lord Daglum would arrive.

Sophia placed her hand over her queasy stomach and took another deep breath. Was Mr. Fawcett the reason for her discomfort? It had been four weeks since she had last seen him in London, but it felt like only a few days ago. Although she hadn't missed him as much as she'd hoped she would, she *had* missed him a little—or rather, his company.

Perhaps all she needed to do was look upon him. Once she saw his kind eyes and welcoming smile again, she would be very glad indeed.

Yes, that was precisely what would happen.

The front door opened, startling Sophia, but when she spied the butler ushering in her parents, she smiled in relief. Her father had insisted that he and her mother stay in the comfort of their own home for the duration of the party and drive over for the various activities, including dinner this evening. Their timing couldn't have been more fortuitous. Now Sophia wouldn't have to enter the drawing room late *and* alone.

"Mother. Father. How are you?"

"I see you are late as well," said her mother, shooting

her husband an accusatory glance. "Mr. Gifford's valet fell ill, and he was forced to tie his own cravat. It took him ten attempts to produce that sorry knot."

Sophia's lips twitched. The knot was sorry indeed. She walked over to her father and fiddled with his cravat, pulling a little here, straightening there, and doing her best to make it look less sad.

"I think we are all fashionably late, with Father being the most fashionable of us all," Sophia at last declared with a pat to his chest.

He craned his neck to see what she'd done, then dropped a kiss on her forehead. "Thank you, dear girl. You have saved me from being an embarrassment to your mother."

Sophia's mother examined the neck cloth and gave a grudging nod of approval. "Much better, Sophia. Now, let us go in before fashionably late becomes unforgivably late."

The butler preceded them into the room and announced their arrival. Sophia looked around, searching for Mr. Fawcett, but the first gentleman her gaze landed on made her forget all about her London suitor.

Curly, dark hair, matching eyes, and a solid, average build. There was something so familiar about him, like a distant memory. When he caught her staring, he smiled, and his lips formed a single word.

*Sophie.*

Only one person had ever called her that. Could it possibly be . . . "Hugh?" The whispered question was out of her mouth before she could rethink it.

His smile widened, revealing a small dimple in his left cheek and crinkling the corner of his right eye a bit more than his left. In that instant, Sophia could see the boy she'd once known in the man who stood before her, and my, how handsome he'd become. Gone were his long, gangly arms and too-thin face, and in their places were a strong jawline and a body that filled out his jacket well. She fought the urge to rush forward and throw her arms around him.

That was something the young Sophie would've done. She was Sophia now—a mature woman who behaved with decorum.

"At last you are here, Soph," said Prudence. "I was beginning to wonder what had detained you."

Sophia forced her attention from Hugh to her sister, but try as she might, she couldn't concentrate. "I, er . . ." Why was Hugh here? Did he have business with Lord and Lady Bradden, or—what, exactly did he do now? To her, Hugh had always been the solicitor's son.

Knave stepped forward. "I would like to introduce an acquaintance of mine. Mr. Quinton, this is my mother- and father-in-law, Mr. and Mrs. Gifford, and my sister-in-law, Miss Sophia Gifford. Mr. Quinton is here at my invitation."

Sophia couldn't mask her surprise. Hugh was here to stay, at least for a few weeks? Why hadn't she known? She had seen the guest list, and nowhere had Mr. Hugh Quinton's name been written. Sophia would have noticed.

"How do you do, Mr. and Mrs. Gifford?" Hugh gave them a curt bow before taking Sophia's hand and smiling at her with affection.

"'Tis a pleasure to see you again, Miss Gifford." His voice sounded different. Deeper, yes, but there was no trace of his old, lovable burr. At some point during the last decade, he'd cultivated a well-spoken accent—not aristocratic, but pleasant nonetheless.

Her fingers tingled where he touched her, and her heart began thumping irregularly. Goodness, what was wrong with her?

*'Tis only the shock of seeing him again,* she told herself.

"Do you know this gentleman, Sophia?" asked her mother.

"Yes," she answered, though it sounded more breathless than confident.

"As do I," said her father in a frigid tone. "Tell me, Mr. Quinton, how did you come to be acquainted with Knave?"

Hugh opened his mouth to answer, but Knave beat him to it. "We have a mutual friend in Lord Rigby."

"Oh? And how do you know Lord Rigby?" pressed her father, apparently determined to uncover how the son of his former solicitor could claim a friendship with both a viscount and an earl.

"Mr. Wycliffe introduced us, sir," said Hugh, naming a distinguished gentleman. When he turned back to Sophia's father, his expression changed from warm to cold in an instant.

Her father appeared ready to demand how Hugh had come to know Mr. Wycliffe as well but seemed to think better of it and clenched his jaw instead.

Sophia stepped in front of Hugh to protect him from the ire that seemed to radiate from her father's entire being. Years ago, she hadn't been brave enough to stand up for Hugh, but she was not as timid now.

*He is my friend,* she silently told her father, *and you will treat him as such.*

Her father grunted and looked away—not surrendering, per se. He was too stubborn for that. But at least he would postpone his interrogation for another time.

Sophia exhaled before turning back to Hugh. She had to admit that she, too, wondered how Hugh had come to be here. A friend she'd once been forbidden to associate with now stood with her as an equal.

She glanced at her sister and Knave. They didn't seem at all surprised by the turn of events. In fact, her sister looked almost gleeful. Good heavens. Was this another of Prudence's matchmaking attempts? Had she somehow discovered Hugh's whereabouts and invited him to Radbourne on purpose? Did she hope an old friendship between children would blossom into something more?

No. Her sister would never.

Except she would. When Prudence felt she was in the right of something, she would do anything.

Oh dear. Here came Mr. Fawcett now. How very awkward. Honestly, how could her sister put her in this position with no warning?

"An honor, Miss Gifford." Mr. Fawcett took her hand and bowed over it. He wasn't the most handsome man she'd ever met. His skin was a little too pale for her liking, and his shoulders too narrow. But he was tall, confident, and didn't have any airs about him. She liked that.

"Thank you, Mr. Fawcett. I trust your journey was uneventful?"

"Merely tedious, as all journeys can be. But I am here now, with you."

Sophia blushed slightly before looking back to Hugh. "And your journey, Hu—er, Mr. Quinton?"

One side of his mouth curved slightly, as though he'd noticed her slip. "Other than an encounter with a highwayman two hours outside of London, uneventful."

A few gasps sounded, and Sophia stared at him, trying to gauge if he had been in earnest. His eyes twinkled merrily, taking Sophia back to a conversation they'd once had as children.

*"If I were to ever be accosted by a highwayman, I hope he'll be devilishly handsome," said the eleven-year-old Sophia.*

"What does that have to do with anything?" returned fourteen-year-old Hugh.

"When he sees I have no jewels worth stealing, he'll wish to steal a kiss instead, and I could never allow an ugly highwayman to kiss me."

"He wouldn't get the opportunity to try," said Hugh gallantly. "I'd relieve him of his weapon first, his horse second, and his pride third."

"Indeed? Do demonstrate." Sophia snatched a stick from the ground and held it out as if it were a sword. "Ho there, sir," she cried. "I demand you give me your money and trinkets or your life."

Hugh focused his gaze on something above her head and pointed. "That poor bird. I think its wing is injured."

"Where?" Sophia spun around, but before she could say anything more, the stick was pulled from her grasp. She glared back at a grinning Hugh, who now directed the stick at her.

"You made that rather easy," he said.

"That doesn't count," she returned. "You know my partiality for animals, but you wouldn't know the same of a stranger."

"Perhaps not, but by distracting you, I would distract him, and the end result would be the same."

Sophia lifted her chin. "What if I am not there to cause a distraction?"

"There would be no need to save you from a blackguard's kiss. I would simply hand over my money and trinkets."

She'd found much to like in his words and laughed. "You, sir, are ridiculous."

"And you, Sophie, are too kindhearted. An injured bird indeed. I could have said an injured ant, and you would've forgotten all else to aid the sorry creature."

"I find it unfair that you know my weakness, but I don't know yours."

"I think you do," he insisted.

She puckered her brow, thinking over all the moments she'd spent with him, but try as she might, she couldn't recall one weakness. Hugh could swim, fish, climb, and even build a tiny boat from the twigs and leaves of an oak tree. He'd always seemed so adept at everything.

"Will you give me a clue?" she asked.

He pressed his lips together for a moment before replying. "Only one. Your answer lies in our story of the highwayman."

Sophia brightened. He'd given her a riddle, and she loved riddles. "Which version of the story? The one where you, or rather I, cause a distraction, or the one where you hand over your valuables?"

He cocked his head and tapped her nose with his finger. "I said only one clue, and I have given it. You will not get anything more from me than that."

"But—"

"No buts. You must figure it out on your own or always wonder."

During the fortnight that followed, Sophia had made several guesses, but none had been correct. In the end, her dear friend was sent away, and she was left to mourn his loss. After that, trying to uncover his weakness no longer mattered, and she'd all but forgotten the incident until his mention of the highwayman with that endearing twinkle in his eye.

"Did he threaten your life?" Prudence asked, obviously interested to hear more. She was always on the lookout for any adventure or inspiration she could use in her novels.

"He trained a pistol in my direction, but I seriously doubt he intended to use it. His hand shook as though he'd never held a weapon in his life, and he appeared ready to faint. The lad couldn't have been more than fifteen."

"Poor boy," said Sophia, picturing the scene and wondering what had driven him to thievery.

"I wouldn't call him poor," Hugh said dryly. "He made off with my gold pocket watch and purse, which happened to contain a significant amount of money."

"You allowed him to rob you?" Mr. Gifford scoffed, obviously unimpressed that Hugh couldn't outwit a frightened youngster.

"Yes," Hugh answered, catching Sophia's eye. "I didn't have a friend along to distract him."

*He did remember,* Sophia thought, feeling a flush warm her cheeks.

"Surely you could have overpowered the boy," said her father.

"And risk getting shot? I think not," said Hugh. "Besides, he looked as though he hadn't had a decent meal in weeks. I couldn't bring myself to deprive him of his loot."

To think Hugh had once called *Sophia* too kindhearted.

"Did you send word to the nearest magistrate?" Mr. Fawcett asked. "I should hate for other travelers to befall a similar fate."

"I did not," said Hugh.

"What were you thinking?" Sophia's father looked at him in disgust. "He may be attacking another as we speak."

"Perhaps," said Hugh with a curt nod. "Or perhaps he decided to take the money, clean himself up, and call upon my friend in London who happens to be looking for an employee with his skill set. I gave the lad his card."

"You are friends with a man who wishes to hire a thief?" cried Sophia's father.

Her mother's expression was equally horrified. "What sort of friend is this?" She may as well have accused, *What sort of person are you?*

"A jewelry merchant. He is always on the lookout for brave couriers to transport his more valuable wares across the country. He pays handsomely and makes it well worth their while."

"Didn't you say the boy's hands shook, and he appeared ready to faint?" Sophia couldn't help but inquire.

Hugh answered with a small smile. "He still went through with it, didn't he? In my opinion, that makes him more courageous than most. Besides, he didn't seem to care for thievery, which was another reason I gave him a different option should he choose to take it. My friend will give him the training he needs to be a successful courier."

Her father harrumphed, her mother scowled, Mr. Fawcett appeared thoughtful, Prudence grinned, and Sophia was reminded of why she'd thought so well of Hugh Quinton.

But that had been so long ago. Who was he now? What sort of man had he become? He'd once been the son of her father's solicitor and a dear friend. Now, he claimed a friendship with a viscount, an earl, a jewelry merchant, *and* a thief.

Sophia ached to ask about his life and what had brought him to this point, but not with so many ears listening. She wanted privacy for that conversation. Perhaps they could take a stroll through the gardens after dinner or . . . no, that could never happen. There was now Mr. Fawcett to consider, and judging by the determined look in her father's eyes, Sophia would be hard pressed to exchange pleasantries with Hugh, much less enjoy a *tête-à-tête*.

Gone were the days she and Hugh could sneak away to race makeshift boats down a stream.

With a glance in Mr. Fawcett's direction, Sophia had to concede that perhaps her parents would be right to discourage her away from Hugh. After all, Sophia had not invited her London suitor to watch her become reacquainted with an old childhood friend. Mr. Fawcett was her future and Hugh her past. She'd do well to remember that.

When dinner was announced, Mr. Fawcett was quick to approach her. "Would you be so kind as to accompany me?" he asked.

She forced a smile and placed her hand on his arm. "'Twould be my pleasure, sir."

# FOUR

AFTER A BRIEF knock, Sophia walked into her sister's bed-chamber and closed the door. Prudence sat at her secretary, writing frantically with her pencil, while her Yorkshire terrier, Scamp, lay bored at her feet.

Sophia cocked her head. "Didn't you promise Knave you would set aside your scribblings for the duration of the house party?"

Prudence held up her free hand to stop Sophia from talking further and wrote another sentence or two before looking up.

Her long, dark curls hung around her shoulders in a slightly haphazard way, as though she'd removed the pins and left it to fall where it pleased. With the candlelight flickering across her face, she had an eccentric look about her. Sophia bit back a smile.

"I am not writing. I was only making some notes about a story that struck me earlier this evening. If I don't record the ideas when I have them, I forget, and this was too delicious of a tale to let slip away."

Sophia wished she'd taken the time to change and re-move the pins from her own hair, although her untamed, flaming-red curls would likely make her appear even more eccentric than her sister. But Prudence looked so cozy in her nightdress, while Sophia felt anything but.

She'd come here after being waylaid by her mother, who'd made it very clear that Sophia was not to fraternize with the son of their former solicitor, regardless of his current social status. It seemed Sophia's father had found the time to enlighten her mother about the newcomer's true identity.

Sophia dropped down on her sister's bed and rested her head against a pillow, too tired to hold herself up any longer. It had been an emotionally taxing day. Her body ached to crawl under the soft bedclothes and let sleep overtake her, but her mind would not be quieted until she'd spoken with her sister.

"Does your new story involve a highwayman, by chance?" Sophia asked.

Prudence propped her elbows on the desk and placed her chin in her palms. "You know me too well. I couldn't help but be inspired by Mr. Quinton's recounting of that young, frightened boy. It's a story begging to be told."

"I knew you'd think that," said Sophia. "I'm actually a little surprised you didn't immediately excuse yourself to, er . . . record your notes."

"I very much wanted to, but I refrained. You should be most proud."

Sophia fingered the fringe around her sister's pillow, her mind on other things. She tried to make her voice sound as nonchalant as possible as she asked, "Speaking of Mr. Quinton, why did you not tell me he'd been invited?"

Before Prudence could answer, the door that adjoined her bedchamber to her husband's opened, and Knave walked in. His cravat had been cast aside, along with his boots, and the top two buttons of his shirt were undone. Sophia felt her face grow warm. She might have excused herself, if not for the fact that she had a few questions for him as well.

"I heard voices and figured I'd investigate." He seemed to notice the pencil in his wife's hand and pointed a finger. "You promised."

She dropped the pencil as though it had burned her and held up both hands. "Only note-taking, my love. I am still a woman of my word."

He rolled his eyes, then bent to kiss her cheek. "She can't help herself, can she?" he said to Sophia. "I'll wager her so-called notes have something to do with the highwayman."

Sophia snickered and Prudence pouted. "Am I that predictable?"

"Yes," said her husband and sister in unison.

Prudence stood and wrapped her arms around her husband's waist, looking up at him. "I was only note-taking."

"Something tells me there will be much more of that between now and the end of the house party."

"Perhaps a little more, but not *much* more."

He chuckled, pulled her closer, and kissed her forehead. "I'm holding you to that, my love."

Sophia tried not to be jealous of the pair, but sometimes it was difficult to push the feeling aside. Her younger sister had the very thing Sophia had craved for three long years. While Sophia loved them both dearly—two people couldn't be more deserving of happiness than they—it was difficult to witness their obvious affection while knowing she'd never have the same.

When Knave caught Sophia watching, and undoubtedly noticed the pained look on her face, he quickly released his wife and cleared his throat, then smiled ruefully at his sister-in-law.

Prudence picked up Scamp and came to sit on the edge

of the bed, near Sophia's feet. "Sophia is wondering why I didn't tell her that Mr. Quinton would be joining us for the party. I was just about to explain that it had been you who had issued the invitation, not me."

"How do you know him, Knave?" Sophia finally voiced the question that had been on her mind all evening.

He shrugged and sat on the corner of his wife's desk, folding his arms. "I don't, really. Our acquaintance doesn't go beyond two months ago, and our interaction since that time has been sparse, to say the least. What I do know is that he's made quite a name for himself among the upper crust, helping many to rejuvenate their fallen estates and turn them profitable once again."

Sophia wasn't sure how to take this information. "I don't understand. Why would he do that?"

"Because they pay him handsomely," Knave explained.

"So he's in trade." It was more of a statement than a question, but Knave nodded nonetheless.

"I see." Sophia twisted the pillow's fringe around her finger. She didn't know why the news felt like a letdown. It wasn't as though she'd considered the possibility that something *could* actually happen between them. But it was difficult to swallow nonetheless.

"Is Radbourne in trouble?" she asked, her voice noticeably smaller than before.

Knave exchanged a brief look with Prudence, and only after she gave her nod of approval did he say, "No. Talford Hall is."

Although his words made Sophia lift her head and tuck her legs beneath her, the revelation didn't come as too much of a shock. Her parents had tried to keep the truth from her, but any fool would notice their attempts to economize over the past few years. All but a few of the servants had been dismissed, and though it had never been voiced aloud, she was certain that Prudence and Knave had put up the blunt for Sophia's three seasons. Even her abundant dowry had come from Knave's father, as part of the marriage settlements between his son and Prudence. Knave had wanted Sophia to have her pick of London suitors.

If only it had worked out that way.

Sophia pushed her self-pitying thoughts aside. Was there truly a chance she'd lose the only place she'd ever called home?

"The estate is no longer profitable, Soph," said Knave carefully, "and your father doesn't know how to reverse the situation. I encouraged Hugh to come as my guest and, while here, look into things."

"Does Father know why he has come?" Sophia asked. He'd seemed as surprised as she to find Hugh standing in Lord and Lady Bradden's drawing room.

"Considering their history, I thought it best not to reveal the true nature of his visit."

Another wave of disappointment rippled through Sophia. For whatever reason, she'd assumed that Knave and Prudence had invited Hugh on her account—a final attempt to save Sophia from a loveless union. How silly to think such a thing. Hugh was not here to renew an old acquaintance. He'd come to help her father and mother—two people who couldn't be less grateful.

Sophia slid her weary body from the bed. "I take it Hugh isn't really friends with Lord Rigby and Mr. Wycliffe?"

Knave shrugged. "It's more of a business friendship, but he is well-respected by those he's aided. The man is nothing short of a miracle worker when it comes to estate management. From what I understand, he's done quite well for himself, though you would never know it by the frugal way he lives."

"I do hope he can help Talford," said Sophia, though her voice sounded flat. Somewhere inside of her, a light had dimmed. It was probably just exhaustion.

She paused at the door to add, "It was good of him to come all this way for a man who once treated his family so shabbily."

"That's not why he's here," said Knave.

"Why then?"

"Sophia, Sophia." Prudence kissed her dog and set him down on the bed next to her. "How naive you can be sometimes."

Sophia thought it best not to voice her confusion, although she was certain her expression conveyed it clearly enough.

"Knave only had to mention the estate would one day fall to you, and that's all the convincing it took." Prudence walked over and put her hands on her sister's shoulders. "He's here to help *you*, Soph. Only you."

Sophia blinked as a swirl of happiness swelled within. Her old friend had returned to Lynfield because of *her*. She had always wondered if she had left as lasting of an impression on him as he had on her, and now . . . well, perhaps she had.

The knowledge didn't really change anything. Hugh was still a solicitor's son and she a gentleman's daughter, but as Sophia walked back to her room in a bit of a daze, her steps were lighter than they'd been all day.

# FIVE

THE FOLLOWING AFTERNOON, Abbey and Brigston arrived with their little girl, Anne, and Brigston's mother, the dowager Lady Brigston. They were ushered into the great hall, where Sophia descended the stairs to find them looking harried and exhausted.

"How good it is to see you all," she said warmly, giving them each a hug. When she spied Abby's eighteen-month-old daughter asleep in her mother's arms, she added quietly, "Hello to you too, little Anne."

The child's curly blonde locks and ruddy cheeks made her look like a cherub. How wonderful it would be to have a toddler running about for the duration of the house party. At times, Sophia wondered why Prudence and Knave hadn't yet been blessed with a child of their own, but she'd never dared broach the subject with her sister.

"It was a tiring ride, I see," Sophia whispered.

"You have no idea," said Abby as she handed her baby to the nurse. "Anne didn't care for the last half of the ride and didn't try to withhold her feelings."

"That's putting it mildly," muttered Brigston. "I was on horseback next to the carriage, and her shrieks could still be heard. I was ready to leave her at the last posting inn and return for her when she was in a better temper."

"Fiddlesticks," said his mother. "You adore that child, shrieks and all, and would never do anything of the kind."

"Perhaps not, but if we had been more than a few hours away from Radbourne, I might have secured a room at an inn for Abby and myself and sent you ahead with Anne."

"Now that I *would* believe," said his mother dryly, making Abby and Sophia laugh.

"I'm certain you will want to wash up and rest before dinner," said Sophia. "Come, and I will show you to your rooms. Prudence and Knave must have been waylaid in town, so you will have to wait until dinner to see them. Catherine will also be here, along with Mr. Fawcett, Mr. Quinton—a childhood friend of mine—and Lord Daglum."

"Lord Daglum!" Abby cried, then immediately lowered her voice. "You must be joking. Prudence would never invite him."

"No, but our mother would—and did, unfortunately."

"Drat," said Abby with a grimace. "He will make things decidedly less enjoyable. But at least Catherine will be here."

"Agreed," said Sophia. Catherine Harper, a close friend, had chosen to remain at her estate not far away, but, like Sophia's parents, she planned to participate in most of the activities.

"I suppose you ought to show us to our rooms straight-away," said Abby. "If I am to greet Lord Daglum with any sort of civility, I will need to be well rested."

"In that case, perhaps I should rest as well," said Sophia as she led the way up the stairs. "You must promise that if you see Lord D corner me, you will find a way to save me. Mother is still set on us marrying."

Abby looped her arm through Sophia's at the top of the stairs. "I can't, for the life of me, understand why, but don't worry. I'll be there for you."

WITH HUGH, MR. FAWCETT, and Lord Daglum all at Radbourne, dinner was a harrowing affair. Sophia spent the hour in the drawing room before trying to divide her attention equally between Mr. Fawcett and Hugh, while doing her best to avoid Lord Daglum. Her mother made the latter impossible when she suggested he accompany Sophia in to dinner.

Their entire conversation, if it could be termed one at all, consisted of hearing about Lord Daglum's many hunting, horse racing, and gambling exploits. When he wasn't speaking, he was eyeing Catherine or the pretty maid in the corner as though they were large slices of cake.

Sophia did her best to listen, but her mind—and gaze—continually strayed in the direction of Hugh. What had he said to make Catherine laugh? Mr. Fawcett and the dowager Lady Brigston also seemed entertained by his words, judging by the way they grinned. Sophia envied them all. But at least her parents had opted to ignore Hugh, rather than engage him. That was something to be grateful for.

To her relief, the plates were eventually cleared away, and she was allowed to return to the drawing room. Once there, Catherine immediately approached Sophia. With her rich auburn hair, well-endowed figure, and emerald silk gown, it was no wonder she drew the attention of Lord Daglum. Moments such as those made Sophia grateful she would never be called a beauty. It was bad enough having to speak to the man. If he were to ever look at her as he did Catherine, she'd likely cast up her accounts.

"Brute is still behaving beautifully, thanks to you," said Catherine. "He hasn't uprooted any more of my flowers, he comes when he is called, and he no longer barks at innocent puppies."

Sophia smiled. The two women had gotten to know one another a few years prior when Sophia helped Catherine better understand her misbehaving dog. After the death of Catherine's husband, the large mastiff became unruly and mischievous. Catherine was ready to be done with the dog—at least until Sophia stepped in to help.

Now all was well, it seemed.

"I am glad to hear it," Sophia said. "He's a spirited creature but also has such a tender heart. I grew very fond of him."

"As have I, and thank goodness, too. Stephen would have rolled over in his grave had I sent that animal away." Although Catherine smiled, she couldn't hide the underlying sadness in her eyes. It appeared every time she spoke of her late husband, and Sophia wondered if it would ever fade completely. How difficult it must be to go on without him.

"I wish you had joined us last season," said Sophia.

Catherine made a face. "I have no wish to reenter The Marriage Mart. I was blessed to have a wonderful union, brief as it was, and could never look at another man without comparing him to Stephen. He made sure that if anything happened to him, I could live comfortably on my own, and I find that I'm quite content."

They stood apart from the rest of the party, but Sophia still lowered her voice. "Do you get lonely?"

"Of course. But I prefer to live alone than with a man I cannot love."

Sophia's gaze drifted to Mr. Fawcett, and a heavy feeling pressed against her chest. Prudence often spoke of love, as did Abby, and now Catherine, but what did it mean to love a man? Did Sophia love Mr. Fawcett, at least in part? Could she grow to love him more? Would she find happiness as his wife, or would she spend the rest of her life dissatisfied and regretful?

It wasn't as though he would make her *un*happy—he was too kind of a man to ever do that—but Sophia would likely never feel the kind of bliss spoken of by her friends and sister. Could she be content with such a marriage, or was she better off alone, like Catherine?

The sorry fact of the matter was that Sophia would never really be alone. Catherine had the luxury of being financially independent whereas Sophia would never see a farthing of her dowry if she didn't marry. Even then, it would be controlled by her husband. And if she remained unattached, she'd be at the mercy of her family, forced to remain with her mother and father or continue to prey upon the charity of Knave and her sister.

These were the sort of thoughts that often plagued her mind—thoughts that kept her encouraging Mr. Fawcett, discouraging Lord Daglum, and trying not to think too much of Hugh. Though her heart was definitely drawn to him, social status was a gulf too wide to breach, no matter how much she might wish to dip her toes in the water.

"Mr. Fawcett is a kind man," Catherine commented, no doubt following Sophia's gaze. "He reminds me a little of my brother."

"Does he?" Sophia had never met Catherine's brother, but she'd always spoken highly of him.

She nodded. "Quiet, but also witty. He's very easy to be around, isn't he?"

"Yes." Sophia had never thought of Mr. Fawcett as particularly witty, but he did have a calm demeanor about him. She'd always appreciated that aspect of his character.

"What are you lovely ladies discussing in such a secretive fashion?" intruded a grating voice that made Sophia's skin prickle. She had been forced to listen to that man during all of dinner. Could she not have at least a little respite?

Catherine was kind enough to respond. "I was telling Sophia how much I despise hunting. Do you not think it a barbaric pastime to kill animals?"

"Only useless animals. It isn't as though we're hunting thoroughbreds." He chortled as though he'd made a clever joke, but Sophia was certain even Catherine would agree that Lord Daglum wasn't the least bit witty. If Sophia was forced to put up with his company for much longer, she'd start blurting out some very unladylike things.

Hugh materialized at her side with Mr. Fawcett not far behind.

"Miss Gifford," said Hugh, "I was just wondering what you think of the poem, 'To a Louse' by Robert Burns? Have you read it?"

"Robert Burns?" Lord Daglum scoffed. "Never say you actually read the rubbish he writes, Mr. Quinton. He's nothing more than a baseborn Scot."

"I do, actually, and have found much to like in his words," answered Hugh smoothly.

*Bravo*, Sophia thought. She only knew one Robert Burns poem—"A Red, Red Rose"—and only because her sister had quoted it often over the years. But she had learned to appreciate it, which surely gave her enough of an opinion on the matter to agree with Hugh.

"As do I," she said.

Mr. Fawcett was more honest in his response. "I only know one or two of the man's poems, but they were both thought provoking. Tell me about this louse business, Mr. Quinton."

Apparently Lord Daglum had no patience for poetry written by a Scottish man of low birth because he quickly excused himself, much to Sophia's relief.

She gave Hugh a look of gratitude, and he returned it

with a sly smile. "Might I suggest that you continue to study more of Mr. Burns' poems, if only for your own defense?"

Sophia was hard pressed not to laugh, and judging by the way Catherine's eyes danced, she felt the same.

"I shall begin at once," said Sophia.

"I also overheard Lord Daglum say he has no patience for silly parlor games, or any games without stakes," added Mr. Fawcett in a low voice.

"Perhaps if he comes around again," said Catherine, "we'll suggest a game of charades."

"For now," Sophia added, "I am content to let him speak with my mother." Her father was busy glaring at Hugh. Why her parents detested him, she had no idea. He may not be their equal, but he was far more likable than Lord Daglum.

"He probably wouldn't care for riddles, conundrums, or Bouts-Rime either," Hugh added.

Sophia gave him a grateful smile. All day, she had worried how she would manage interactions between the three gentlemen, but she needn't have worried at all. Not only did Hugh and Mr. Fawcett seem to get along well, they'd only just made it clear that she would not be alone in her efforts to keep Lord Daglum at bay.

If only her mother would realize that he would make a dreadful husband as well.

"Perhaps a game of charades is in order right now," murmured Catherine. Sophia followed her gaze to see that Lord Daglum had moved on to Abby and Prudence, neither of whom looked overly pleased to converse with him.

"Agreed," said Sophia, waving Prudence over to make the suggestion.

Her sister was easily convinced, and a game of charades was soon formed. After only one round, however, Sophia's parents took their leave. Perhaps all that glaring had given her father a headache.

Lord and Lady Bradden and the dowager Lady Brigston followed soon thereafter, and only one round after that, Lord Daglum pled exhaustion and escaped as well. Sophia settled back in her chair, perfectly content with those who remained. Hugh seemed to relax as well.

At the front of the room, Mr. Fawcett examined the phrase written on the piece of paper he'd been given and held up four fingers.

"Four syllables?" asked Sophia at the same time Catherine called out, "Four words?"

He gestured to Catherine that she had guessed correctly, then began to walk about the room in a feminine fashion, swinging his hips, batting his eyelashes, and preening. Amidst the laughter, Sophia and Hugh called out several guesses, but it wasn't until Catherine leapt from her chair and blurted, "'She Walks in Beauty,'" that he stopped and grinned.

"Well done, Mrs. Harper. You've guessed it."

Sophia and Hugh hadn't even come close.

"You make a dreadful woman," said Hugh as Mr. Fawcett took his seat.

"I consider that a compliment," he replied, making everyone laugh.

Smiling, Sophia looked around the room. Knave, Prudence, Abby, Brigston, Hugh, Mr. Fawcett, Catherine. This was the first time since the house party had begun that she'd been able to relax and enjoy herself. It felt wonderful.

A throat cleared behind Sophia, and she turned to see the butler standing in the doorway.

"Please forgive the intrusion, Lord Knave," his deep voice resounded, "but a missive just arrived by courier for Mr. Fawcett."

Mr. Fawcett rose immediately, his brow furrowed, and quickly broke the seal. He glanced over the letter's contents before refolding it and tucking it into the pocket of his coat.

"My sister has taken ill," he said. "She has asked that I leave as soon as possible to attend to her. As it is only the two of us and my aunt now, I feel I must go."

Sophia rose to her feet as conflicting feelings assaulted her. There was fear for his sister—she must be very ill to be in such urgent need of her brother—along with concern for herself. If Mr. Fawcett left, how would her family become better acquainted with him? How would she? Sophia had so hoped that if he won over those closest to her—Prudence in particular—she would feel greater confidence in accepting his suit.

Chiding herself for her selfish thoughts, Sophia stepped towards him. "Of course you must go, Mr. Fawcett. Please convey our wishes to your sister for a speedy recovery."

"Will you be able to return, do you think?" Prudence voiced the question that Sophia longed to ask.

"My sister didn't give many details, but I shall try my best. 'Twould be a pity to miss all of the excitement."

His gaze came to rest on Sophia, and he took hold of her hand. "I had hoped to become better acquainted with your family. Please forgive me for leaving in such a rush. I shall return as soon as I am able."

Sophia's cheeks heated at the way he singled her out. "There's nothing to forgive, sir. I wish you and your sister well and hope we will see you again soon."

He nodded, thanked Prudence and Knave for their hospitality, and quit the room.

An awkward silence descended, and Sophia wasn't sure how to fill it. She looked to her sister for help.

"Pity," said Prudence. "I was beginning to like that man. Can we not send Lord *Brag*lum away instead?"

Sophia's lips twitched, as did several others. Her sister's frankness endeared her to many but shocked many more. Thankfully, none of the latter were present.

"Did I hear you correctly?" Sophia asked, taking a seat once more. "Did you just say you were beginning to like Mr. Fawcett?" She ought to feel thrilled, or at least relieved, that her sister was finally coming around, but confusion continued to tumble to and fro inside her, like fallen leaves on a windy day.

"Oh, he has always been a likeable creature, I suppose," said Prudence, "but it was fun to see a humorous side to him this evening. If only Mother and Father hadn't retired early. Perhaps they would have enjoyed his theatrics as well."

"I don't understand why your mother wishes you to wed Lord D," Abby said. "The man is a complete boor and Mr. Fawcett a dear."

Sophia's cheeks heated even more as she glanced at Hugh. He stood with one elbow propped on the mantle, his face a blank canvas. She could only imagine what he must be thinking. He was likely wishing he'd retired earlier with her parents.

Ah well, nothing for it now. Her problems were out in the open, a spectacle for all to see.

She forced her attention back to Abby. "Mother sees what she wishes to see and ignores what she doesn't."

"What, precisely, does she wish to see?" Hugh asked, surprising Sophia by joining the conversation.

"Prestige, mostly," she answered. "Mother believes that's all it should take to make one happy."

"Only because it's something she's always desired but has never had," added Prudence.

Brigston discarded his coat on the back of the sofa and took a seat at his wife's side. "As much as we'd all like for

Lord Daglum to leave, it's probably a good thing he remains."

Everyone looked at him as though he'd sprouted elephant's ears, even his wife. Sophia might have laughed if she hadn't disagreed. Who, in their right mind, would wish for Lord Daglum to stay?

Abby patted her husband's knee in a maternal manner. "Perhaps you should take yourself off to bed, my love. You're speaking nonsense."

He smiled. "How else will Mrs. Gifford come to see Lord Daglum as he truly is? Surely, we can find a way to remove her blinders in the next fortnight."

"And, with any luck, elevate Mr. Fawcett's standing at the same time," added Abby, looking at her husband in pleased delight. "Brigston, you are a genius."

"I have my moments," he said, leaning back with his hands behind his head.

Sophia smiled, but she didn't really mean it. Her friends could always be counted upon to come to her aid, but how did they hope to achieve such a miracle? Mr. Fawcett would always be a mere gentleman, and Lord Daglum a marquess. That was all that mattered to her mother.

"Is Mr. Fawcett connected to a title at all?" asked Brigston. "A distant relative, perhaps?"

Prudence shook her head. "Mother would have found a connection if it existed. When it comes to a suitor's pedigree, she is quite thorough."

"Perhaps we could invent a relative," Catherine suggested then frowned. "No, that's a terrible idea. Lies have a tendency to go very wrong. Hmm . . . I really have no idea what to do. Mr. Quinton, I understand that you are a man of unique stratagem. What do you propose?"

Hugh seemed momentarily caught off guard, but then

he shrugged. "Well, I suppose if you want to influence some-one who values standing in society above all else, you must make Mr. Fawcett appear the better choice."

"Yes," said Abby. "But how do we achieve that?"

Hugh pushed away from the mantle and took a seat on the settee next to Sophia. She immediately felt the warmth of his body, smelled the pleasing scent of sandalwood, and wished for him to come a little closer.

He studied her a moment before saying, "What if another contender were to enter the fray—say a man of low standing, like myself—and we succeed in proving Lord Daglum the lout that he is. Next to me, I believe your mother would have reason enough to think Mr. Fawcett a very good prospect, wouldn't you agree?"

Silence enveloped the room as everyone digested the idea—everyone except Sophia, that is. With Hugh so near and those dark, probing eyes on hers, she couldn't digest anything. Her mind whirled, her heart pranced, and her breathing became shallow. One would think she'd suffered an apoplexy.

"I like it," Prudence's voice finally cut through the mayhem in Sophia's mind. "Mr. Quinton, you *are* a man of stratagem. I can't think of anything better than having you court my sister."

Sophia's eyes widened as her mind began to grasp what was being said. Hugh? Court *her*? She frantically thought back to what he'd said. Something about a man of his stand-ing and Mr. Fawcett . . . Oh no. Hugh couldn't possibly be serious. It would be better to invent a fictitious relative than have two people feign a romantic interest in each other—or rather, *Hugh* feign an interest in her.

Sophia needed to put a stop to this now.

"He was only jesting Pru," she blurted. "Isn't that right, Hu—er, Mr. Quinton?"

Before he could answer, Prudence said, "Jesting or not, it *is* a wonderful idea. Would you be willing, sir?"

"I wouldn't have suggested it otherwise," he said, directing a smile at Sophia.

At a loss for words, she looked to Abby for help. Surely her friend would realize nothing good could come from such a scheme. Hadn't she only just pointed out that lies had a tendency to go very wrong?

*Please, say something,* Sophia's eyes pleaded with hers.

Abby cleared her throat. "I believe we're forgetting about Lord Daglum. As Mr. Quinton mentioned, unless we find a way to lower his esteem in Mrs. Gifford's eyes, any untitled gentleman will appear lacking. Should that not be our focus at present?"

*Bless you,* Sophia thought—until her sister waved Abby's words aside with a flip of her wrist. Prudence's eyes gleamed in that stubborn way that told Sophia her sister's mind was set.

Drat.

"I believe both should be our focus. After all, it's only a matter of time before Lord *Brag*lum reveals his true, boorish self to Mother and she comes to her senses. Don't you agree, my love?"

"If I didn't, would that dissuade you?" Knave answered wryly.

"No."

"Then I see no reason to disagree."

Sophia glared at her brother-in-law while those around her laughed, Hugh included. Knave shrugged and settled back in his chair, offering Sophia nothing more than a look of sympathy. The coward.

"Pru, why the sudden interest in aiding Mr. Fawcett?" Sophia blurted without thinking. Up until now, her sister had been insistent that Mr. Fawcett wasn't the right man for Sophia. Had he managed to win her over already? Was her sister truly sad to see him go?

"I am not interested in aiding *Mr. Fawcett*. I'm interested in aiding *you,* dearest. You still prefer him to Lord D, do you not?"

Once again, Sophia felt her face turn an unattractive shade of red. She knew this because any shade of red looked dreadful against the backdrop of her orange hair. Why did Prudence have to be so blasted forthright at times?

"I believe we all do," she finally said, wishing she had a fan. "But I do not think—"

Prudence clapped her hands together, cutting Sophia off. "Then it's settled. Mr. Quinton will begin to show a romantic interest in Sophia—which you must return, Soph—and the rest of us will see that our resident pompous lord becomes a mere peasant in Mother's eyes."

Sophia stared at her sister. How could the matter be settled when it hadn't been properly discussed? Did no one care about *her* feelings on the matter? Could no one see how this fiasco might affect her? The last thing Sophia needed was a fictitious suitor, especially if that suitor happened to be Hugh.

No, this wouldn't do at all.

"As I was saying," said Sophia, more firmly this time. "Mr. Quinton came here as a kindness to our family. I will not ask anything more of him than that."

Hugh leaned a little closer, and Sophia could feel his breath on her cheek. "You didn't ask, Miss Gifford. I offered."

Her unruly heart leapt, and Sophia wished once more for a fan. Hugh was supposed to be a man of sense and stratagem. Could he not foresee the consequences of this plan?

Although the thought of him pursuing her sent delightful chills through her body, it wouldn't be real, and Sophia knew she wouldn't walk away unscathed. How long had it taken her to push his memory aside all those years ago?

Too long. Just seeing him at Radbourne nearly undid her. If he began to pay court to her, it may very well be her undoing.

Apparently, he didn't share her same feelings or concerns. From the look on his face, he was as taken with the plan as her sister. Perhaps to him, she would only ever be a good friend.

"Miss Gifford," he said, "would you do me the honor of accompanying me on a ride tomorrow morning?"

Sophia had to force her gaze to his. How she despised the formal use of her name on his lips. It sounded stiff and unfriendly, as though he'd forgotten the close connection they'd once shared. She was being ridiculous, of course. After all, he couldn't call her Sophie anymore than she could call him Hugh, but it still felt wrong somehow.

"A ride sounds lovely," she finally mustered. For now, she'd let them all think she intended to go along with this ridiculous scheme. Come morning, however, when her sister was no longer present, Sophia intended to make her old friend reconsider.

# SIX

THE OVERCAST SKIES looked questionable when Sophia and Hugh set out for their morning ride, a bored-looking groom trailing behind.

"I think it might rain," Sophia said, frowning at the gray clouds overhead.

"You sound like that is a bad thing, but I have a vivid memory of you twirling and laughing in the rain."

Sophia detected a hint of his old country burr, as though he'd lowered his guard. It made her smile, along with the fact that he remembered that day in the clearing. She remembered it as well. They had gone walking in the woods, searching for worms to use as fish bait, when a storm rolled in. As the first droplets fell from the sky, Hugh had taken off his jacket and held it over Sophia's head.

*"We must get you back home before you're soaked,"* he said.

*The skies opened then, and rain tumbled down. He looked so stricken that Sophia had laughed.*

*"A little rain never hurt anyone."* She ducked under his jacket and ran into a clearing, filled with the sort of happiness only Hugh could inspire. She tilted her face to the sky, opened her arms wide, and spun.

*He laughed as he joined her. Through the pounding rain,*

*he executed an awkward bow and raised his voice above the sound of the rain.* "Will you dance with me, Miss Gifford?"

"I'd love nothing more, sir," *she quipped and took his hands. Having just left the school room behind, a few years his junior, Sophia hadn't yet learned the steps to any dances. Neither had Hugh. Solicitors' sons didn't exactly frequent dances. So they made the steps up as they went, tripping and laughing all the while.*

It had been one of those perfect moments Sophia had never forgotten. How she'd love to dance with him now. Had he ever learned how?

"A little rain never hurt anyone, I suppose," she said, cocking her head at him.

"No indeed."

They set off across the meadow, and Sophia urged her horse into a fast clip. The wind whipped at her face and hair, further elevating her spirits. If she'd been alone, she would have removed her bonnet and let her hair fly from its pins. She loved the feeling of freedom that came on the back of a horse. There was no one around to tell her what she should wear or how she should comport herself. No one chided her on being too quiet or not encouraging eligible gentlemen. No one said anything about her red hair or freckles. And no one weighed her down with talk of love.

As she reached the other side of the meadow, she glanced back to see Hugh not far behind. How handsome he looked in his tan buckskins and dark jacket. He had a confident, unconcerned way about him that put her at ease. He didn't seem to care that his father was a mere solicitor nor did he cow in the company of people like Lord Daglum. She found that aspect of his character appealing, probably because she had always placed too much stock in the opinions of others.

When he stopped beside her, his expression contained admiration. "Lord Knave didn't exaggerate when he said you were an excellent rider. I shouldn't be surprised—you were always a quick study when we were younger—but I have never seen a woman ride as you do, with equal parts grace and abandon."

It was a rare thing for Sophia to be praised in such a genuine, unabashed way. The few times she had been, she'd been too flustered to offer a sensible response. But with her old friend, it was an easy thing to return his smile.

"Thank you, Hugh. Is it all right that I call you that when we are away from the others? No matter how hard I try, I cannot make Mr. Quinton roll off my tongue. It doesn't sound right. I would love for you to call me Sophie as well."

He grinned. "I had the same thought but wasn't sure you'd condone such familiarity."

She studied him a moment. Dark waves peeking below his beaver. Honest, kind eyes. Firm jaw. Over ten years had passed since he'd been ripped from her life and yet . . . "This may sound strange, but it feels as though hardly any time has gone by since I've last seen you. No, that's not right. It feels an age since I've seen you. I have missed you dearly. But . . . well, I'm not sure how to explain."

"Do you mean to say that our friendship feels as easy now as it did years ago?" he guessed, his eyebrow quirked.

"Yes, that's it exactly." Even as children, he'd always understood her. Was it because he felt the same?

"Shall we walk a bit?" he asked.

"I'd like that."

Sophia swung her leg over the pommel, removed her foot from the stirrup, and slipped from Dominicus just as Hugh came to assist.

He chuckled. "You always did like to do things on your own."

She ducked her head. "Forgive me, Hugh. In the country I am accustomed to mounting and dismounting without help. We employ only one stablehand at Talford, and he is not usually nearby when I wish to ride. With a mounting block I manage just fine."

"You saddle your horse as well?"

"More often than not."

"Of course you do," he murmured, chuckling again. He didn't offer his arm, only gathered his horse's reins in his hands and fell into step beside her. Apparently this feigned courtship would only occur when they had an audience.

"I've been told you've come to help my parents—or rather, our estate," she said.

"I've come to help *you*, Sophie," he corrected.

The warmth in his expression, combined with his words, made her stomach flutter and chirp, like an enthusiastic little bird. Ridiculous. One would think she was a silly chit just out of the school room.

"I intend to look over the ledgers this afternoon. Lord Knave said he'd have them for me after luncheon."

"Would you mind if I joined you?" Sophia hoped he wouldn't think it too brazen of a request. But she would one day inherit the estate, and she would very much like to know where her family's holdings stood. Perhaps she could even be of some help.

He gave her a sidelong glance. "I wouldn't mind in the least, but aren't you expected elsewhere? Lady Knave mentioned something about an outing to town last evening."

"Oh, blast. You're right," said Sophia with a frown. "I take it you won't be joining us?"

"Not if I am to complete the task I came here to do. I must set aside some time for business matters."

Sophia bit her lower lip, picturing herself trapped in a

60

coach with Lord Daglum and her mother for a long, tedious ride into town. Her mother would undoubtedly do everything in her power to foist Lord Daglum upon her daughter in the most irritating of ways. Sophia could already hear her mother's voice. *Is this ribbon not a perfect match to Sophia's eyes? What do you think of this bonnet, sir? Isn't it most becoming on my daughter?*

Lord Daglum would be agreeable, all the while admiring the other, far prettier women in the shop.

Sophia would prefer to spend the afternoon with Hugh.

"No need to look so worried, Sophie," said Hugh. "You are more than capable of handling Lord Daglum."

"It's not him I'm worried about. It's my mother. When she sets her mind to something, she can be quite persistent, and her mind is currently set on me making a match with that man."

"We'll just have to make her rethink the intelligence of her mindset."

He made it sound so simple, as though a whispered word or two would have the desired effect, but Sophia knew her mother better than that. It would take something akin to a miracle to make her cast aside the possibility of a title for her eldest daughter.

"How do you propose we do that?" Sophia asked dryly.

"I have a few ideas." A twinkle appeared in his eyes, and he winked at her. "As your most devoted suitor, I consider it my duty to save you from unsavory characters."

"Such as highwaymen?" she teased.

"Precisely."

"I never did figure out your weakness, you know."

He laughed. "It's because you're too humble. My weakness was you, obviously. I suppose it still is, considering I am here now."

Sophia forgot to breathe for a moment. He'd said it so casually, as though he'd made a comment about the weather or the landscape. But for her, it hadn't felt casual. With most people, she was ordinary Sophia Gifford. Hugh, on the other hand, had always made her feel extraordinary, like she was something special.

She slowed to a stop and ran her gloved fingers along her horse's neck, not knowing what to say. *You're my weakness too* would sound trite, even if it was true.

She chose the safe response. "You didn't have to come, Hugh. You don't owe me anything."

"And miss out on my first summer house party? I think not." He nudged her arm with his. "Besides, I had a feeling you'd need a fictitious suitor to save you from your latest scrape."

She smiled, grateful he knew how to lighten the mood and remind her that he hadn't meant anything serious with his confession. He cared for her as a friend, nothing more.

"Speaking of this suitor business," she began, "I think—"

"That it's a brilliant idea?" His tone was teasing, as though he knew she didn't think anything of the sort.

"Er . . . not exactly."

He stepped next to her and took the reins from her fingers. "What is wrong with my plan, Sophie? Is the thought of me setting my sights on you so distasteful that you can't even pretend an interest in me?"

"Heavens no," she said.

"Then what?"

Perhaps she should have rehearsed this conversation in her mind a few more times. With his handsome eyes trained on her, only a breath or two away, Sophia was finding it very difficult to think clearly.

"It's as Abby said yesterday. Lies have a tendency to go very wrong. I simply don't feel comfortable with the plan."

"With the plan or with me?" He leaned in closer, his mouth threatening a smile.

"Drat it all, Hugh, you already know I'm comfortable with you. I just don't like the idea of pretending." This conversation was not going at all how she'd hoped. If only he'd retreat a few steps and not smell so deliciously of leather and sandalwood. And did he have to keep smiling at her in that charming, irresistible way?

"What if I'm not pretending?" His grin widened into a devilish smile.

Sophia had no idea what to say to this. She stared at him, wide-eyed, her pulse leaping from one rapid beat to the next like a frightened grasshopper.

"I'm only teasing, Sophie," he said, his smile falling away. "No need to appear so nervous."

"I'm not nervous."

"What did you just say about lying?"

She felt a blush heat her cheeks, and she had to refrain from rolling her eyes. "So you agree we should not go through with this farce."

"I never said that."

"But you were thinking it?" she asked hopefully.

His lips twitched, and he shook his head. "No."

Sophie sighed as she tugged her horse's reins free from his grasp. "What can I say to make you change your mind?"

"That you will marry Mr. Fawcett regardless of your mother's wishes—assuming that is your desire."

"I . . ." Sophia's voice trailed off. How could she make such a promise when the mere thought of marrying Mr. Fawcett sent a wave of panic through her? Goodness, what was the matter with her? She'd never felt this anxious about him before. Confused, perhaps. Wary. Not downright fearful.

Hugh grabbed his horse's reins just below the bridle and nodded in her direction as he pulled his animal forward. "That is why I intend to show an interest in you, Sophie. I'll not see you unhappy. You must insist on marrying the man you wish to wed. If it is Mr. Fawcett you want, I will see to it that it's Mr. Fawcett you get."

He began walking again, and Sophia could only stare after him. She should tell him that she *would* insist on marrying the man of her choosing and had no problem sending Lord Daglum packing if it came to that. She should probably also tell him that she wasn't sure about Mr. Fawcett either.

But that might lead to more questions—questions Sophia wasn't ready, or willing, to answer.

*Oh my giddy aunt,* she thought. *What a muddle.*

Hugh paused to look back at her. "Coming?" he asked.

She forced her feet forward, pulling her horse along. As she fell into step beside him, she decided it would be better to leave well enough alone for now. "One would think *you* were the marquess and not Lord Daglum. You are more of a gentleman than he will ever be."

"Yes, well, I have spent a great deal of time around the upper class and have learned a thing or two over the years."

"Don't even think of giving others the credit, Hugh. You have always been a man of honor. 'Tis a shame that confidence, intelligence, and gallantry can only get one so far."

He cast her a sidelong glance, and she detected a glimmer of hurt in his eyes. "However far I've come is far enough for me, Sophie. I have no aspirations to become anything more."

Oh dear. Without meaning to, she'd offended him. "I didn't mean it like that."

"How did you mean it?"

She gave the matter some thought, only to finally shrug. "Perhaps I did, although it was meant to be a compliment."

"I know. A person *should* want to elevate his social standing—only an idiot wouldn't care for such things—yet here I am, claiming to be such an idiot."

He dodged around a few low-hanging branches and made sure his horse did the same. "As I said before, I've spent a great deal of time among the gentry, and if there is one thing I've come to understand, it's that I don't want that sort of life. To always be concerned about the thoughts of others, having to fret over matters of fashion, and feeling like I need more of one thing or another to maintain a certain appearance—no, that is not the life for me."

Now it was Sophia who felt a little insulted. "It is not always like that. Take Prudence and Knave, for example. They don't give a farthing for what the ton thinks, and Abby and Brigston are the same. Their families and close friends are enough for them, and—" Sophia stopped when she thought of Knave and his parents, who purchased some of Talford's lands years ago so they could hold the claim of being the largest landowner in the province.

Hmm . . . perhaps not even Knave was immune to the desire for increased wealth and status.

Hugh picked up her hand and held it securely within his own. "I shouldn't single out your class. It's a struggle all people face, no matter their station—even me, for all my self-righteous claims. It just seems that the higher a person advances, the more frivolous their concerns. There are exceptions, of course, but I've seen enough to believe that your mother's mentality is more commonplace than your sister's. Is that fair to say?"

"I suppose." But it left Sophia to wonder where she fit

into it all. Were her desires too frivolous in nature? In some ways yes, in others, no. She was certainly not willing to marry Lord Daglum just to obtain a title. The question that plagued her the most, however, was where did *Hugh* think she stood?

There she went again, worrying about the thoughts of another. But surely it wasn't a bad thing to crave the good opinion of someone you respected.

He pressed his finger against the space between her brows, where her worry lines manifested. "You are wondering if I consider you one of the frivolous group, aren't you?"

Her eyes snapped to his. How did he do that?

"I think," he continued without waiting for her to respond, "that you are in a class of your own, Sophie."

His fingers grazed her cheek and his expression held warmth, implying he'd meant it as a compliment. With anyone else, she might have found a reason to believe otherwise, but this was Hugh—a man who'd never spoken an unkind word to her.

He smiled and dropped his hand from her face. "That's more like it. No more worry lines."

Sophia couldn't resist smiling. "I have to wonder, sir, who taught you how to charm a lady? If memory serves, you've always had a knack for it. Your father, perhaps? No, he had more of a brooding nature if I recall. It must have been your mother. Was she a lovely, kindhearted soul?"

"The kindest and happiest woman I've ever known." His expression became thoughtful. "My father didn't always brood about, you know. He mourned the loss of my mother for years—probably still does. After she passed, a light went out in our lives."

Sophia knew it had been a struggle for Hugh and his father. Mrs. Quinton was a woman who had been dearly missed, a person Sophia would have loved to know. But at the same time, if she hadn't passed away, the elder Mr. Quinton wouldn't have brought his son to Talford Hall, and Sophia would have never met Hugh. It felt wrong that the greatest hardship for the Quintons had been a blessing to her.

"What became of your father?"

Hugh didn't answer right away. He pulled a branch from a tree and began plucking small leaves from its stem. "After that summer, your father saw to it that his reputation was never the same. He lost nearly all his clients, and we were forced to move to London and begin anew. It took time. I had to put schooling on hold to help earn a living, but he eventually acquired new clients and rebuilt his good name."

Sophia stared at him. She'd had no idea her father had brought ruin upon the elder Mr. Quinton, nor did she know they'd had to move away from Hugh's childhood home. She'd only witnessed the man's abrupt dismissal and felt the loss of a dear friend.

"Oh, Hugh, I am so sorry." She put a hand on his arm, looking up at him. "If my shoe hadn't gotten stuck in the mud, if I would have given up on it sooner, if my father had been kinder, or if I had not been so selfish about your time, wanting to spend every moment I could sneak away with you, none of that would have happened."

He collected her hand between both of his and smiled. "I have never wished for that, not now and not back then. Your friendship has been something I have always held dear. I don't blame you in the least for what happened, and everything came about all right in the end. I only regret our summer was cut short. We never did make it to the top of that large oak."

He was so close she could see the dark scruff along his jaw and the flecks of amber in his dark eyes. How strange she'd never noticed those before.

"You remember the tree?"

"I remember everything, at least everything I can remember." He grinned and released her hand, much to her disappointment.

She chided herself for her wayward thoughts and wondered, not for the first time, why she couldn't feel the same way with Mr. Fawcett—a man she *was* at liberty to marry. Perhaps it was a situation of wanting what she could not have. If Hugh and Mr. Fawcett's situations were reversed, perhaps she wouldn't feel this way.

Sophia tucked her hands behind her back and stepped to the side, ready to resume their walk and evade his disconcerting gaze. In so doing, she snagged her blue velour bonnet on some branches and gasped when it ripped several pins from her hair.

"Blast," she muttered as she untangled it from her hair to inspect the damage. Other than a small tear in the fabric, it appeared to be unaffected.

"Bonnets can be such a nuisance," she said. "I am always snagging them on branches because the brim blocks my view."

"They also hide that lovely shade of hair." He picked up a strand that had come free from her knot and tucked it behind her ear. She tried not to react to his touch but some things couldn't be helped.

"Lovely?" she asked wryly. "I think you mean appalling."

"Unusual, perhaps," he conceded, "but I think that's why I like it so much. It sets you apart."

"And my freckles? Do you like those too?"

"As a matter of fact, I do. They're charming."

"And you, sir, are doing it a bit too brown."

He glanced at his horse, who stood grazing a few feet away. After a time, he said, "Tell me, Sophie, how did you come by those freckles?"

She gave him a wry smile. "I already told you. I detest bonnets."

"So you defy that particular social custom and hang the consequences."

"Only in the country," she confided.

"That," he said, pointing a finger at her, "is why I think your freckles are charming."

Sophia blinked at him, feeling fluttery all over again. *That is your gift, isn't it?* she thought. *You look beyond the outside of a person and see what's inside. You find beauty because of who they are, not what they are.*

There weren't many men like Hugh. Yes, Mr. Fawcett also admired Sophia for the person she was, but instead of finding beauty in her red hair and freckles, he seemed to dismiss them as a minor inconvenience. Hugh viewed them as assets.

"What do you say we do what you'd like to do most?" Hugh proposed.

She tucked her bonnet under her arm and squinted up at him. "What, pray tell, is that?"

He removed his beaver and tossed it on a nearby boulder, then held out his hand for her bonnet.

"Gallop without hats or bonnets. Come now, hand it over."

She grinned and immediately capitulated, feeling giddy and lighthearted. "I would like nothing more."

"I know." He set her bonnet next to his hat and gave her a leg up. In no time at all, they were flying across the meadow. Sophia's knot in her hair loosened, and several strands of hair whipped at her face. She felt a surge of euphoria as she leaned low over Dominicus and let the horse run to its heart's content.

The groom who'd been charged to keep an eye on them struggled to keep up, and by the time they had circled the meadow and cut back through the woods to where they'd left their hats, the poor man was some distance behind.

Sophia laughed in delight. Normally, she only rode that way on her own, but today it had been better with a friend.

"Thank you, Hugh," Sophia said as she pinned her bonnet back in place. "That was the most fun I've had in a long time."

"For me as well."

# SEVEN

As Sophia feared, she was directed into the same barouche as her mother, her father, and Lord Daglum. She attempted to hide her envy as she glanced over at the neighboring carriage, containing Abby, Brigston, Prudence, and Knave. They would undoubtedly have a delightful drive, whereas she would undoubtedly not.

Catherine, being an intelligent woman, had cried off from the activity altogether, as did Knave's parents and the dowager Lady Brigston.

As the carriage started forward, Lord Daglum asked Sophia, "How was your ride this morning?"

She blinked at him. He'd never bothered to inquire about much of anything regarding her before, so the question came as a bit of a shock.

"I spied you returning from the stables with Mr. Quinton," he added a bit stiffly.

"What's this?" her father growled, obviously not pleased she'd been seen riding with a man he detested. Her mother held the same opinion, judging by the look of displeasure on her face.

Sophia was actually glad she'd upset them. Hugh's revelations that morning left her completely out of charity with her father, and because her mother insisted she ride

71

with Lord Daglum, she didn't feel much goodwill for her either.

"It was enlightening," Sophia said, in answer to Lord Daglum's question.

"Oh?" His dark eyes gleamed with interest. Although he sported a similar eye color to Hugh's, Lord Daglum's seemed malevolent, somehow, like she was looking into the eyes of a snake. He probably assumed she had unflattering gossip about Hugh to share, which conveyed how little he knew her.

"I discovered Mr. Quinton is a wonderful rider," she said. "I do hope we can go again sometime."

Lord Daglum frowned, her father's eyes narrowed, and her mother's jaw clenched. Good. Let them stew on that for the remainder of the drive. As far as Sophia was concerned, they deserved any insubordination she could inflict on them.

"If you enjoy riding that much, I would be happy to join you on a morning gallop," Lord Daglum said. "Zephyr is the fastest mount in the stables—as well he should be for as much blunt as I paid for him last year."

The man's thoroughbred was a beautiful one, Sophia had to admit, but it also seemed to prance and preen like its master.

"I'm not sure I'd be able to keep up with you."

"Not to worry, Miss Gifford. I always slow down for the ladies."

Sophia shot her mother a look. *Is this really the man you'd like me to marry? He's patronizing, arrogant, and irritating.*

Even her mother seemed annoyed by his answer. "No need to take it easy on Sophia. She is an excellent horse-woman."

Lord Daglum nodded half-heartedly, as though he

didn't believe any woman capable of keeping up with him or his prized Zephyr. "If you are such an adept rider, Miss Gifford, than you must enjoy hunting. It's too early in the season for foxes, but I hear we are to hunt pheasants in a few days."

He shared the same opinion as many in their station— the reason Prudence had planned the excursion—but that didn't mean Sophia would participate. It was one thing to eat pheasant. Another to watch a helpless bird being shot from the sky.

"I'm afraid I share Mrs. Harper's opinion," she said. "I cringe at the thought of an innocent bird being shot. Or a fox, for that matter."

"Come now, Miss Gifford, surely you jest. Foxes are a nuisance and should be hunted. The fewer of them in the world the better."

Sophia had to bite her tongue to keep from saying, *The fewer Lord Daglums in the world the better.*

"Be that as it may, I prefer to root for the fox."

Her father chuckled. "Sophia has always had a soft spot for animals."

"She certainly has a way with them," agreed her mother. "I can't begin to count the number of animals and their owners she has aided over the years. If Zephyr ever misbehaves, it is Sophia you should look to for help. She's a wonder."

Sophia's heart softened a bit, and she even smiled at her mother. Even though the praise was meant to turn the head of an infuriating marquess, Sophia appreciated it nonetheless. It wasn't often she received compliments from that quarter.

Lord Daglum sniffed and peered out the window. "Zephyr wouldn't dare to misbehave."

"Oh? Why is that?" Sophia asked.

"Because he'd get a sound lashing."

His words and the coldness in which they were spoken twisted Sophia's stomach. Suddenly his horse didn't seem as prideful as it had before. The poor animal had a beastly master.

"You whip your horse, sir?"

He seemed to realize his answer had garnered her distain and quickly amended, "Of course not. There has never been a need. Zephyr has always behaved as he should."

*If your wife doesn't behave as she should, would you whip her?* Sophia thought callously. Just when she thought she couldn't despise Lord Daglum more, he proved her wrong. Lord *Brag*lum didn't do his character justice. He was more deserving of a title befitting a truly odious man, like Lord Dodious.

Yes, that would work.

Once in town, her feelings were reaffirmed when she caught his lustful gaze following a voluptuous woman walking along the side of the road.

Odious indeed.

Of course her parents were completely oblivious.

Prudence and Abby tried their best to steal her away from Lord Dodious, but her mother constantly found a way to steer her attention back to him or his to her.

"Lord Daglum, wouldn't this bonnet look lovely on Sophia?"

"Sophia, isn't Lord Daglum so very clever?"

"Oh my, what a handsome pair you make."

Sophia couldn't refrain from rolling her eyes at this last remark. Truly, it was the most trying afternoon she'd spent in a long while.

When they finally arrived back at Radbourne, and she

found Catherine cozily ensconced with Hugh in the drawing room, laughing heartily at something he'd said, Sophia's mood darkened further. Wasn't Hugh supposed to be poring over ledgers or whatnot?

With barely a nod of greeting, she excused herself and escaped to the solitude of her bedchamber, where she was surprised to see that it was still only two-thirty in the afternoon. How was that possible? It felt like they'd been in town for hours and hours.

Thinking she'd been given a small miracle, Sophia quickly donned her riding habit for the second time that day and trotted down the back stairs to the stables. She needed something to clear her head and elevate her mood, and a good hard ride was the only sure way to do that.

SOPHIA CRINGED AT her reflection in the looking glass one last time before leaving her room. She'd briefly considered pleading a headache and excusing herself from dinner, but a spirit of rebellion carried her down to where the others had already gathered in the drawing room. The moment she spied her mother's expression of shock, she steeled herself for the onslaught.

"Sophia, your face!" her mother cried. All others looked her way, and Sophia had to force her feet to remain where they stood.

Earlier that afternoon, she'd spent over two hours in full view of the sun, either riding or laying in an open meadow, plucking small yellow wildflowers and blades of grass. It had been unusually warm, and the sun on her face had felt wonderful.

Only when her skin began to sting did she realize her

mistake—and the reason for her mother's anger now. Her burned skin clashed dreadfully with her hair, and it was only a matter of time before more freckles appeared. Not even her lovely gold evening gown could temper the ghastly shades of red.

Sophia lifted her chin, refusing to be cowed by her mother's look of horror. After such a trying afternoon with Lord Dodious, Sophia could only hope her appearance would make him reconsider pursuing her. The addition of a few more freckles would be a small price to pay, though perhaps she shouldn't have stayed in the sun for as long as she had. Her skin would undoubtedly begin to shed soon.

Prudence slipped her arm through Sophia's and pulled her to the side of the room. "Burning your face is extreme, Soph, even for you. Are you that worried about Lord Humdrum?"

Prudence and her names. It was almost enough to make Sophia smile, but not quite.

"I cannot abide him, Pru. If Mother requests that he take me into dinner again, I will revolt. I will stare her down and say, 'Absolutely not. I would rather have my entire body burned at the stake than spend a moment longer in that man's company.'"

Prudence chuckled. "Bold words, my dear."

"I mean every one of them."

"I believe you."

From the corner of her eye, Sophia caught Catherine exchanging whispered words with Hugh. He nodded in return. Apparently, the two had become as thick as thieves. How perfectly wretched. In that moment, Sophia wanted to call an end to the house party, return to Talford, and spend the remainder of her summer in peace. Only it wouldn't be that peaceful with her mother on the premises.

Hugh grinned at something Catherine said, and Sophia's stomach clenched. *You are supposed to be courting me, not my beautiful friend,* she thought, then immediately rebuked herself.

Honestly, what was the matter with her? She had never felt so out of sorts. One would think she'd been drinking or some such nonsense. Her thoughts should be on Mr. Fawcett, not Hugh. She needed to stop obsessing over her plight and remember that the others didn't deserve to have their evening spoiled by a rotten mood.

When Hugh and Catherine finally approached, their eyes glinted in amusement.

"Is it very painful?" Catherine asked.

"Not at all," Sophia lied. To her recollection, she'd only burned her face this badly once before. As a child, she'd escaped the nursery while her nurse snoozed in her chair. Sophia had run outside, thinking it would be a great game to hide in the gardens. It had been a chilly day, but the sun had heated her skin, so she'd reclined on a bench to bask in its warmth while she waited to be found.

Eventually she had fallen asleep, and when a frazzled and worried maid had finally stumbled upon her, there was no undoing the damage to Sophia's face. A day or two later, her skin began to peel and sun spots appeared.

Her mother had been horrified then, just as she looked horrified now.

Hugh, thank goodness, didn't try to comfort Sophia with insincere flattery about her appearance. He merely bowed over her hand and asked if she'd do him the honor of accompanying him to dinner.

"Lord Daglum has asked to take me in," Catherine added under her breath.

Sophia should have been thrilled by this turn of events,

but it seemed unfair that Catherine—or anyone, for that matter—should be made to endure Lord Dodious's company in her stead. To make matters worse, it seemed as though Hugh had invited Sophia only because the beautiful Catherine was no longer available.

"I'd be honored, sir," she said stiffly.

He gave her an odd look, which was perfectly understandable. She'd walked into the drawing room with a fiery face and a temperament to match.

"Catherine was just telling me how you saved her dog," he said.

Sophia wanted to groan. That's what they'd been discussing? She'd been so certain the pair had been flirting. But no, Catherine had been singing Sophia's praises instead.

What a nitwit Sophia was. She really ought to have stayed in her room this evening, perhaps even for the duration of the house party.

"Brute didn't need saving," she clarified. "It was simply a misunderstanding."

"Don't be so modest," said Catherine. "You gave me something of Stephen's back, and I will always be grateful to you for it. That dog has become very dear to me, and I would have found him a new home if not for you."

"I'm undeserving of such praise," said Sophia with complete honesty. After her earlier uncharitable thoughts, she deserved nothing.

Catherine opened her mouth as if to argue, but the butler cut her off by announcing dinner. Thank goodness.

Sophia slipped her arm through Hugh's and tried to relax. But it was no use. His touch unnerved her, and combined with everything else, she felt jittery and anxious. It didn't help that her parents looked ready to protest the table arrangements.

As Sophia took her seat, she caught a glimpse of her face in a mirror hanging on the wall across the table and tried not to wince. Merciful heavens, she looked dreadful.

"Forget your face, Sophie," Hugh whispered as he pushed in her seat. "The redness will subside in a few days."

"Do you speak from experience?"

"I may not have the freckles to show for it, but this face has seen its share of the sun. There are times it benefits me to look like I've spent time working in the fields. Tenants tend to speak more freely when I'm not a pale-faced toff, as my manservant would say."

She smiled. "At least you probably still look handsome with a red face."

His eyes twinkled as he took the seat at her side. "Do you think me handsome, Sophie?"

The question should have embarrassed her, but she found herself nodding truthfully. "I have always thought so, yes."

When color brightened his cheeks, her smile widened. "Never say I have put you to the blush, sir."

"Not at all." He looked down and took his time spreading his napkin across his lap.

"Pity," she quipped. "I was hoping that, as my friend, you'd find a reason to continually blush throughout the night, so I'll not be the only red-faced person in the room."

His shoulder brushed hers as he leaned in close. "Red face or not, you will always stand out in a room full of people."

Sophia's stomach flipped and flopped. He could have meant that in many different ways—awkward people stood out, odd people stood out, unattractive people stood out—but the warmth in his gaze told her it had been a compliment. My, she was growing to adore this man.

As opposed to the previous evening, dinner seemed to fly past. Conversation flowed, Sophia's laugh echoed through the room more times than she could count, and her face actually began to ache from smiling. The only time her happiness dimmed was when she glanced in Catherine's direction and saw her friend trying to look interested at something Lord Dodious said.

*Bless you,* Sophia thought guiltily. *It should be me with him and not you.*

Catherine looked up and caught Sophia watching her. She made a comical face and smiled. *I'm fine,* she seemed to say. *Forget about me and enjoy your evening.*

Someday, Sophia would find a way to properly thank her friend.

Once they'd adjourned to the drawing room following dinner, Catherine, Abby, Brigston, Prudence, and Knave all congregated around Sophia and Hugh, asking to know what had been so humorous at dinner.

Sophia couldn't tell them any particular thing. Many of the jokes had stemmed from their youthful escapades. She couldn't possibly explain.

Hugh seemed at a loss for words as well.

It was a relief when Lady Bradden began sorting through some sheet music at the pianoforte. "What about a musical number?" she asked. "I already know Prudence plays beautifully, but what about one of the other young ladies? Sophia, Abby, Catherine? Would any of you care to play?"

"I'm afraid my talents on that instrument are sadly lacking, my lady," said Abby.

"Mine are extremely rusty as well," Catherine quickly added. "I'm certain Sophia would be the better choice."

"I'm certain I am not," said Sophia, wishing she had been the first to speak up.

Hugh chuckled. "Come now, Miss Gifford, you can't be all that bad."

"Perhaps not, but I am not all that good either."

Everyone watched her expectantly, and Sophia began to panic. Oh, dear, they didn't believe her. Now what? She really wasn't that good, as Prudence and their mother would attest. Why were they not agreeing with her?

"I believe you are being modest," said Hugh, pulling out the bench for her. "Come now. Show us what you can do."

Sophia shook her head, giving him a warning look. *Must you make me even more of a laughing stock? Cannot the state of my face suffice?*

He must have misinterpreted her expression because he didn't appear deterred.

"Very well," she finally conceded, "but only if you agree to sing, Mr. Quinton. If I recall, your resonant voice is the only sound that can drown out my deficiencies."

She had a vague memory of Hugh once telling her that he couldn't carry a note to save his life, and from the incredulous expression on his face now, she'd been right.

*What do you have to say now?* she thought smugly.

"You sing, Mr. Quinton?" Prudence asked delightedly. "How fortunate! Yes, you must both perform this instant."

Sophia tilted her head up at him and grinned. *If you can give it, be prepared to take it, my friend.*

"I, er . . . Sophia has grossly exaggerated my talents, or lack thereof."

Sophia stifled a giggle.

"Perhaps it would be best if Prudence performed for us," Sophia's mother finally inserted. "She sings and plays beautifully."

"I think I would like to hear Sophia and Hugh," Prudence insisted. "You have piqued my curiosity, and it will not be satisfied until you perform."

Hugh finally gave in and shrugged. "It *is* a nuisance to have one's curiosity piqued. We would be cruel not to satisfy it, eh, Miss Gifford?" A hint of his old burr came through in his voice, and Sophia hid a smile.

He began sorting through the music, apparently not expecting a reply.

*Oh no,* Sophia thought. He really did intend to perform. Had he lied to her all those years ago and he really *could* sing?

Perhaps she should have taken out her earlier frustrations on the keys of the pianoforte instead of on horseback. Sophia honestly couldn't remember the last time she'd practiced. Last year, perhaps? Or had it been two? Her mother had given up encouraging her ages ago.

Hugh finally stopped when he came to a song he seemed to know and held it up for her inspection. "Can you play this?"

"As well as I can play anything." She took the pages from him and sat down, wiggling her fingers in an attempt to loosen them. At least after this embarrassment, no one would ask her to play again.

Sophia managed to get through the introduction without too much trouble, mostly because the notes weren't overly complex. When Hugh's voice joined in, however, she stumbled a little and had to press her lips together to keep from giggling. *Oh, my. He hadn't been exaggerating when he'd said he couldn't sing.*

He sang loudly, as though he had no idea how dreadful he sounded. At one point, his voice even screeched. Sophia made the mistake of glancing at Abby and Brigston. At the look on their faces, she couldn't stop a snicker from escaping her mouth. After a few more measures, she finally gave up and doubled over in laughter.

"You are doing that on purpose," she accused between giggles.

His twitching lips were the only indication he was guilty. Instead of admitting it, however, he gave her a wide-eyed look of innocence. "Doing what on purpose, Miss Gifford?"

"Singing like a goat," she said. "No one sings that badly unless on purpose."

"Sophia Eleanor Gifford!" cried her mother in shocked tones.

"No, no." Hugh held up a hand. "She's right, although I was attempting to mimic a braying donkey and not a goat."

Sophia doubled over again, and the others finally seemed to realize that Hugh had been teasing them all. Laughter sounded throughout the room—coming from everyone except her parents—and Prudence was heard to say, "How delightful. I will have to use this in a book someday, my love. Perhaps the repentant highwayman can also be a poor singer? Oh, Mr. Quinton, can you truly not carry a note?"

"Not in the least." He looked at Sophia. "Forgive me for bringing you down to my level of ineptitude, Miss Gifford."

"On the contrary, sir. You made me sound most adept." And then it struck her. Hugh had done it all for her. He'd made himself the laughingstock to keep the focus off of her. Their gazes locked, and for one magical moment, she saw the truth of it in his eyes.

*How easily I could fall for you,* she thought. Perhaps she already had.

"I must say, Mr. Quinton," said Lord Bradden with a chuckle. "In all our years of entertaining we have never had such an amusing performance within these walls. You are to be commended."

"Perhaps I should take my act on the road," he quipped. "What do you say, Miss Gifford? I'll need an accompanist."

"I'd say that we'd find ourselves without employment and would need to resort to thievery to survive."

"Like that highwayman?"

"Exactly. Only there would be no kind soul to come along and save us."

He seemed to consider her words before shrugging. "Perhaps it would be best to stay as we are and not perform in public again."

"Agreed."

Prudence clapped her hands delightedly. "Oh, Mr. Quinton, I am so glad you have come. You have given me a host of ideas for my stories. I cannot thank you enough!"

Hugh acknowledged the compliment with a bow of his head. "You intrigue me, Lady Knave. I'm rather curious about the nature of these stories. I shall have to read one of them someday."

"There is a copy in the library if you feel so inclined," said her husband. "Call me biased, but I think she's quite talented."

Prudence laughed at that, tucking her arm lovingly through her husband's. Sophia watched the pair, and for once felt no envy. Only gratitude. How lucky was she to have such wonderful people in her life.

Lord Dodious must have grown tired of the conversation because he proposed a game of poker. "The ladies are welcome to join in the fun, of course, unless they have other, more important things to discuss. I realize poker can be a tedious game for the fairer sex."

In other words, he would rather the women not participate. Sophia's hackles rose. It wasn't as though she cared about not being included, but the way he went about it was uncouth. Besides, rumor had it that Lord Dodious preferred games of high stakes—the sort of stakes more suited to a gambling den than a summer house party.

Not surprisingly, her father readily agreed to the suggestion. The other men seemed more hesitant—Hugh even cast a wary glance in her direction—but they eventually capitulated. Sophia watched them go, feeling uneasy. Her father had never been lucky at cards and had lost a tidy sum over the years. She could only hope that wouldn't be the case this evening. Surely Hugh, Knave, and Brigston would make sure the stakes remained inconsequential.

"Mrs. and Miss Gifford," called out Lady Bradden. "Come sit with us. Prudence has suggested we host a soirée on Friday next, and we'd like you to join the discussion."

It was then that Sophia noticed she wasn't the only one who stared worriedly at the empty doorway. With a forced smile, she slipped her arm through her mother's and guided her over to where the others were clustered.

"Do say you'll let me handle the floral arrangements for the evening," said Abby. "I can already picture the ballroom alive with color."

"That would be wonderful," said Lady Bradden.

"We'll want to invite all our friends and neighbors, of course," added Prudence. "It will be a bit of a scramble to pull everything together in the upcoming days, but with everyone's help, I think we can manage."

Sophia forced her mind away from the game happening in the adjacent room and asked. "What can I do?"

Prudence outlined her plans, and all the women took a small task to complete. Lady Bradden would take care of the menu preparations. The dowager Lady Brigston offered to oversee the table arrangements. Prudence would secure the musicians, and with Catherine's help, organize the other entertainments for the evening. And Sophia and her mother would compose the invitations.

Sophia couldn't help but get caught up in the excitement of it all. It would be a beautiful night. She pictured people laughing and dancing and filling the house with life. She pictured herself enjoying the company of family, friends she hadn't seen in a while, and . . . Hugh. She wasn't sure why she placed him in a category of his own. It was wrong. If anyone should be set apart, it was Mr. Fawcett.

Would he be back in time for the dance? Did she hope he would be?

*Of course I do,* she thought firmly.

Talk eventually turned to little Anne and the new words she was learning to say. Before long, Abby and the dowager Lady Brigston excused themselves to look in on their daughter and granddaughter. Sophia watched them go with wistfulness, wondering if she'd be able to give her own mother such a gift some day. Would Prudence? Her sister also gazed after the pair with a sad sort of yearning. Was something wrong? Sophia wondered if she should ask her sister about it. The subject was a tender one.

Those who remained chatted for a while longer until Catherine yawned.

"I believe it's time for me to go," she said with a smile, asking the butler to have her carriage sent around.

Not long after she'd gone, Brigston, Lord Bradden, and Knave returned. When Brigston saw that his wife had gone to check on their daughter, he quickly followed suit. Lord and Lady Bradden made their excuses as well, leaving behind only Knave, Prudence, Sophia, and their mother.

"Lord Daglum had the devil's own luck all evening," Knave murmured to his wife, though his voice carried to Sophia and her mother.

They waited in strained silence for what felt like an eternity before Mrs. Gifford finally rose and rang for the butler. As soon as the man appeared, she said, "Will you please tell Mr. Gifford I am feeling unwell and would like to retire?"

Ten minutes later, her father appeared, his shoulders slumped and face lined. Sophia glanced at her mother. She tried to feign indifference as she pulled her shawl around her shoulders, but she couldn't fool Sophia. They both knew the stakes had been too high.

*Oh Father, how much did you lose?*

She wanted to strangle Lord Daglum—well, all the men, really. Why had they agreed to play? Why had they allowed her father to gamble what he did not have to lose? Hugh had rallied around her only yesterday, devising a plan to save her from Lord Dodious. Couldn't he have done the same for her father?

Where the devil was he, anyway? Still playing? He had never seemed like the gambling sort. As a lad, he'd called it a dull pastime. But it had been ten years since she'd seen him, and time changed people. There was probably a lot she no longer knew about him.

"I'm not feeling well myself," Sophia blurted to her sister. "I think I will say goodnight."

Prudence and Knave nodded solemnly, and Sophia made her escape, dragging her weary body up the stairs.

*How could you, Hugh?* she thought. It wasn't as though she expected him to be perfect. Everyone was flawed in some way. But what he'd done tonight—or rather *hadn't* done— well, it hurt.

# EIGHT

HUGH TUGGED HIS neckcloth free and tossed it on the bed. Quiet snoring came from the other side of the room, and he peered through the darkness to see Park snoozing awkwardly in a chair.

The man could sleep anywhere—and probably had. Though he'd been tight-lipped about his past, Hugh had pieced together enough to know that it hadn't been filled with relaxation or gaiety. Rather, the deep lines etched across Park's face told a story of a man who'd been dealt a difficult hand.

Time and time again, Hugh insisted he didn't need a valet, but his stubborn manservant refused to listen. Park never retired to his own bed before Hugh. When he pledged his loyalty, it was fierce indeed.

Hugh stretched out his aching neck and shoulders, and, as quietly as he could, dressed for bed. Only after he'd finished did he gently shake Park's shoulders.

The man startled awake and leapt from his chair, instinctively moving his hands to a defensive position.

"Relax, Park. It's only me," Hugh said quietly.

Park's hands dropped to his side, and he blinked the sleep from his eyes. When he noticed Hugh was already wearing his nightshirt, he scowled. "What's the point waitin' up for you if you're intent on dressin' yourself?"

"My thoughts exactly. You should've taken yourself off to bed hours ago."

Park's scowl deepened as he dropped back to the chair and ran his fingers through his unruly red hair—hair that was almost the same color as Sophie's. Now that Hugh thought about it, maybe that was one of the reasons he'd liked Park from the beginning. In a small way, Park reminded Hugh of her.

Hugh perched his exhausted frame on the edge of his bed and gazed through the gloom at his one and only man-servant. "I need you to do something for me, Park."

Park seemed to perk up at that, as he always did when Hugh had a special assignment for him.

"I need you to replace one of Knave's footmen for dinner tomorrow evening."

Interest quickly became disgust, causing Hugh to chuckle.

"I'm no footman."

"No, you're not, and you'll undoubtedly make a poor substitute, but I need you to do some sleuthing for me. I'm certain Lord Daglum cheated at cards this evening, but I couldn't figure out how he managed to do it. I need someone I can trust who can observe him undetected, and you're perfect for the job, assuming you can mind your manners."

Park sat up a little straighter, suddenly interested again. "A cheat, eh? Let me at 'im. Always happy to unmask a blackguard."

"I don't necessarily want you to unmask him just yet, just . . . gather information."

Park lifted his hand as though about to salute, then dropped it back to his side and rolled his eyes. "Old 'abits," he muttered.

Hugh studied him for a moment, wondering what sort of demons haunted the man. "You were a soldier," he said, having gathered as much but never voicing his thoughts before now.

"Aye," was all Park said before he rose, signaling he had no wish to discuss it further. Instead, he sighed. "Guess I'll 'ave to dress the part, eh?"

Hugh smiled. From the outset, Park had made it clear he didn't care for uniforms of any kind. He'd once told Hugh he would wear trousers and a white shirt and that was that.

"I'm afraid so, my friend. I'll ask Lord Knave if he can procure you some livery, although we'll be lucky to find anything to fit your frame."

Park grunted, waved a dismissive hand, and slowly walked from the room.

Hugh crawled beneath his bedclothes and let his aching head sink into the soft pillow. As he stared at the shadowy ceiling, he thought back to the day he'd offered the position to Park. It had felt like the right thing to do at the time, but as soon as the tall and gangly redhead had walked out the door, doubt crept in, and Hugh wondered if he'd acted wisely.

Now, two years later, he knew his instincts had been correct. Park was a good man.

# NINE

SOPHIA SECURED HER green velour bonnet with a tight bow and several pins. The sun shone brightly in the morning sky, and she wasn't about to let it cause anymore damage to her skin. She should probably stay indoors for the next several days, but she couldn't possibly go that long without a ride. Besides, Abby and Prudence had asked to accompany her this morning, and Sophia couldn't tell them no. They had much to discuss, which meant the outing turned out to be more of a stroll than a gallop.

"How much did he lose?" Sophia asked the moment they were out of earshot of the stables.

Prudence's forehead creased. "Knave said it was a tidy sum—more than he had to lose. Mr. Quinton returned not long after you went to bed, Soph. According to him, if Mother had not put a stop to it when she did, Father would have wagered his most valuable horse."

"Why didn't Mr. Quinton put a stop to it?" Sophia grumbled.

"What do people find so fascinating about gambling?" Abby asked. "Risk scares me to death."

"I haven't the faintest notion," said Prudence. "The possibility of winning, perhaps? The thrill of instant money?

Knave said the moment Lord Bedlam realized luck was with him, he wasted no time upping the stakes."

"Lord Bedlam indeed," said Abby crossly. "I really do think he's mad."

Sophia felt equally cross. "I hope Father has learned his lesson and will stay away from the tables now." They all knew it was a useless hope. Their father had never exercised restraint when it came to gambling.

"At least Mother didn't seem pleased with Lord Bedlam last evening. First, he had the audacity to take Catherine to dinner instead of you, then he trounced her husband at cards. Perhaps she doesn't think him as great of a catch as she did before."

"Unless she sees an alliance between us as a way of recuperating the loss," said Sophia dryly.

"I have to agree with Prudence on this one," said Abby. "Your mother looked perturbed most of the evening. I'll be curious to see if her demeanor towards Lord Bedlam will be a little less enthusiastic than it was before."

"One can always hope." Sophia's attention strayed to a horse and rider coming through the trees, and she stiffened.

*Hugh.* She mouthed his name without thinking, then frowned when he changed directions and rode their way. It was a strange sensation to have one's heart leap and plummet at the same time.

"Good morning, Mr. Quinton," called out Prudence. "Where are you off to this morning?"

"I've just returned from visiting with some of Talford's current and former tenants." He didn't have the look of optimism about him.

"Former tenants?" Sophia asked, unsure as to why he would have paid a visit to those no longer associated with Talford Hall.

"Your father sold a few farms last year, and I wanted to know how the independents were managing on their own."

"Well, I presume?" Sophia asked.

"Yes. The harvest has been plentiful this year."

"I don't understand," said Prudence. "How does knowing that help Talford?"

Hugh's brow furrowed as he stared off into the distance. "It doesn't. My purpose in visiting was to see if they had taken on too much debt and would be interested in returning the land for the price paid."

Sophia understood his concern well. "I tried to talk Father out of selling those farms, but he'd been determined, assuring me that he could invest the funds in more lucrative ways." What those "lucrative" investments had been, she wasn't sure, but if gambling had been one of them, he hadn't succeeded.

"That hasn't exactly come to fruition, has it?" Hugh said.

Sophia shook her head. "Even if our former tenants were interested in selling, Father couldn't afford to buy the farmland back, could he?"

"Not unless I found an investor." Hugh's tone was less than encouraging. After all, what sort of investor would hand over his money with the promise of little to no return?

None.

*We're going to lose Talford*, she thought.

A lump the size of a grape formed in her throat. Like it or not, she would need to marry Mr. Fawcett. Her dowry was their only hope of not becoming a burden to her sister. Surely Mr. Fawcett would use a portion of the funds to see her parents comfortably situated somewhere.

"My goodness, I'm feeling parched all of a sudden," said Prudence abruptly, waving a hand like a fan in front of her face, as though the weather had suddenly turned miserably warm. "You look a bit flushed as well, Abby. Would you like to return with me?"

"Now that you mention it, tea sounds delightful," Abby answered.

Sophia rolled her eyes at their machinations, especially when her sister went on to say, "Mr. Quinton, would you be good enough to accompany Sophia back to Radbourne when she finishes her ride? She has more stamina than we do this morning and probably wants to enjoy a good gallop."

If anyone had a reason to go inside, it was Sophia with her sun-roasted face. What was her sister hoping to achieve by leaving her with Hugh, anyway? It wasn't as though Sophia wanted to continue discussing Talford's imminent downfall. There was nothing left to be said at this point.

Besides, she was still out of sorts with Hugh for his part in the poker game.

"It would be my pleasure to ride with you, Miss Gifford," said Hugh gallantly.

Sophia gave him a weak smile. "It's kind of you to offer, Mr. Quinton, but I should stay out of the sun."

Prudence's expression turned sour, and Sophia smiled. How satisfying it felt to foil her sister's plans.

Hugh doffed his hat. "In that case, I shall see you ladies at dinner this evening."

The expression on Prudence's face looked almost like a pout. "Will you not be playing nine pins with us this afternoon?"

"Unfortunately, I will be otherwise engaged."

"Oh."

Sophia felt equally disappointed. It made no sense. How could she be upset with Hugh but still long for his company at the same time? One would think it was *she* who belonged in Bedlam.

She forced her head to nod. "Dinner then."

"Yes, and if it is not too presumptuous, would you allow me to be your escort again this evening, Miss Gifford?"

"I . . ." Sophia hesitated. On the one hand, she'd love nothing more, but on the other, she was still angry with him. There was also Catherine to consider. It wouldn't be fair to leave her with Lord Dodious for another night, and . . . well, drat it all, why had Hugh done nothing to extricate her father from the tables last evening? He knew the state of her family's financial situation better than anyone. Unless . . . he still carried a grudge from all those years ago and had enjoyed seeing her father humbled.

"She'd love to accompany you," said Prudence when Sophia remained silent.

Hugh continued to watch her, a question in his eyes. He was waiting for *her* to answer. Her heart melted a little at that.

*May Catherine forgive me.*

"I would love to accompany you, sir," she said.

He smiled and nodded again. "Until this evening then."

She watched him ride away, his back straight, his body swaying in perfect sync with his horse.

The moment he was out of earshot, Prudence demanded, "Why did you not go with him?"

"Why did you want me to?" Sophia countered.

"Because I know how much you love to ride, and Abby and I kept you from a good gallop this morning."

Sophia adjusted her bonnet to keep her tender nose in the shade. "That was thoughtful of you, Pru, but there will be plenty of other mornings to ride."

"Alone, perhaps, but not with an old friend. According to Knave, Mr. Quinton may not have a reason to stay much longer. He hasn't found a way to reverse Talford's situation."

Though Sophia had already ascertained as much, her heart sank at the news—for her parents, her family home, and herself. It would be a difficult thing to lose Talford.

*It will be difficult to lose Hugh too,* came the thought, unbidden.

"Why encourage a friendship that cannot last?" Sophia's voice sounded flat.

"What a silly thing to say," said Prudence testily. "You can be friends with whomever you wish. You can wed whomever you wish. You can become whomever you wish."

Sophia glared at her sister. "If that is the case, why was Hugh cut out of my life a decade ago? Why was I not allowed to communicate with him? Why was he not a guest at any of the parties we attended in London? You're forgetting that we are a class apart, sister, and in England that's a gap that cannot be breached without consequences."

"So hang the consequences!"

Sophia's jaw clenched. It was an easy thing for her sister to say, coming from her position as the wealthy wife of a viscount—an alliance that had pleased all parents involved. Prudence could even write and publish novels without it affecting her standing in society. Yes, there were those who thought it scandalous and looked down their noses at her, but overall, it had given her notoriety, not ostracism. She had become the eccentric Lady Knave, and someday, when her husband inherited his father's earldom, she'd become the eccentric Lady Bradden.

Sophia had a great deal more to lose by hanging the so-called consequences.

"Please stop arguing," said Abby as she struggled to keep her horse from grazing. "If this beast lowers its head any further, I'll lose my hold on the reins."

Sophia let out a frustrated breath. "Forgive us, Abby. By all means, let us return to the house."

They rode in silence for a time before Abby said, "If it helps, Soph, I overheard your mother say that Mr. Fawcett might suit you after all. I don't think she liked how friendly you and Mr. Quinton appeared to be at dinner last evening. I know *I* haven't heard you laugh that much in a long while."

"Nor I," agreed Prudence.

"So you see, our plan is working," said Abby. "Speaking of Mr. Fawcett, has there been any news on the health of his sister or his possible return?"

Sophia bit her lip and furrowed her brow. *She* should be the one wondering about Mr. Fawcett and anxiously awaiting his return. Not Abby.

"No news as of yet," she said.

The moment they arrived back at the stables, Sophia said, not untruthfully, "I feel a headache coming on. Would you mind having my tea sent to my room? I'm going to rest my head for a bit."

"Soph—" Her sister grabbed her arm before she could go far. "I'm sorry. Forgive me?"

Sophia managed a smile. "I can never stay cross with you for long. I shall see you both for nine pins this afternoon."

# TEN

NOT TWENTY MINUTES into the game of nine pins did Sophia wish she'd stayed in her bedchamber with what remained of her headache. The afternoon was as beautiful as the morning had been, with the sun squinting through fluffy white clouds in the sky, but that didn't help her current mood.

Lord Daglum, it seemed, had experienced a change of heart where she was concerned. He began attending to her once again, only with more gusto than before.

"Would you care for a glass of lemonade, Miss Gifford?"

"Why don't you have a seat here in the shade? We wouldn't want to cause additional damage to that lovely nose of yours, would we?"

He even went so far as to inquire about her favorite breed of horse and when she planned to return to London.

Good grief, what had changed? Last evening, she may as well have had the plague with as much notice as he'd given her.

Sophia learned the answer when he took his turn at nine pins, giving her and Catherine a few moments to converse.

Catherine leaned in close, lowering her voice. "You'll have to forgive me for not being able to hold Lord Daglum's attention any longer. Apparently, he'd decided to set his sights on me instead of you, but the moment he learned that

Stephen left me well provided for and that I have no intention of signing my jointure over to any man, should I remarry, he lost interest. The swine. He even had the temerity to tell me that someone with my delicate sensibilities shouldn't want the responsibility of holding the purse strings. Can you believe it?"

"Unfortunately, I can. Thank you for taking him off my hands for at least one night. It was a blessed reprieve."

"Honestly, why can't your mother see him for who he is?"

"I have no idea." Sophia scowled when she spied her mother snagging the man's arm and smiling up at him as though all was forgiven.

"Thank goodness you have better sense," whispered Catherine. "Mr. Fawcett and Mr. Quinton are much more agreeable. Speaking of Mr. Quinton, where is he this afternoon?"

"Locked away in Knave's study," said Sophia, wishing she could be there instead of here. If only she could long for Mr. Fawcett's company half as much as she did Hugh's. Feelings were such peculiar things. They had a will of their own and didn't pay any heed to logic.

"He fancies you," said Catherine.

Startled from her thoughts, Sophia looked at her friend. "Who?"

"Mr. Quinton."

Several emotions stirred within Sophia—joy, confusion, anxiety. How was she to respond?

"He tries to hide it, but over the years I've learned to read people. I'd wager my entire fortune that I am right."

Sophia wanted to believe and disbelieve at the same time. "Perhaps it is *you* he fancies."

Catherine laughed. "I wouldn't mind if he did. The man is quite charming. But alas, it is you who has his full attention. Mr. Fawcett's as well, I believe. The question is, who has yours?"

Sophia was saved from answering by Lord Dodious's return. He flipped up his coattails, nearly whipping her with them, and sat at her side.

She pasted on a smile. "How did you fare, sir? Were you able to knock them all down?"

"Were you not attending?" He appeared affronted that the woman he'd chosen as his future bride—or rather, re-chosen—hadn't paid him any heed.

Too bad she hadn't chosen him in return.

"I'm afraid I was not, my lord," she said, offering no excuses or apologies.

He harrumphed and focused on Abby, who had just rolled the ball towards the pins. It came close but stopped just short of knocking any down. Lord Dodious harrumphed again, probably annoyed that he was being forced to watch the fairer sex perform so poorly. Sophia made a mental note to roll the ball as far from the pins as possible without it being too obvious. By the time her turn came, however, she might be tempted to throw it directly at Lord Dodious instead.

"Miss Gifford," interrupted the butler. "Forgive the intrusion, but a Mrs. Danforth is here to see you."

Sophia puckered her brow. She'd never heard that name before, and had no idea what business the woman might have with her. Not that it mattered. If her arrival meant Sophia would no longer have to endure Lord Dodious's presence, it was a welcome intrusion.

"If you will show her to the parlor, I will be there shortly," said Sophia.

"Er . . . I am not sure the parlor would be suitable, Miss. She has a rather large greyhound with her."

*Ah*, Sophia thought. *She has come to seek my help.* Over the past few years, word of Sophia's talent with animals had spread to the nearby villages and beyond, and many people had brought their troubled pets to her door, hoping for a miracle of some sort. One man had even wanted her to train his goat to not eat his wife's flowers. Some she had been able to help. Others, like the goat, she had not.

Now, it seemed someone had found her at Radbourne. How wonderful that she'd soon have something more useful to do with her time than contemplate throwing a ball at the man seated next to her.

"A woman came calling with a greyhound?" Lord Dodious asked. "Tell her to leave the creature outside. Or better yet, take it home and return alone. What sort of person calls at such an hour anyway?"

"A person in need of help," Sophia said.

The butler appeared concerned. "I can tell her you are not at home to visitors if you wish."

Sophia rose and looked at the butler. "But I *am* at home. If you will show me the way, I would be glad to see her."

A small smile touched the aged butler's face, and he nodded. "As you wish, Miss."

Sophia followed him through the house to the front entrance. On the other side of the open door stood a tall, thin woman wearing a worn, outdated dress. Her face carried the wrinkles of age and hard work, but she had a kind and grateful look about her. Sophia liked her instantly.

"Mrs. Danforth, is it?" Sophia extended her hand in greeting. "I am Miss Gifford."

The woman moved to accept her hand but became distracted when the large greyhound lying near her feet jumped up and began walking in agitated circles, tangling its restraint around her legs.

"Captain, stop that at once," cried the woman, but the dog paid her no heed. He growled at something in the shrubbery and lunged forward, nearly pulling her off her feet.

"Please, Miss Gifford. You must help me. Your friend and my cousin, Mrs. Hilliard, told me you could be of assistance. After observing Captain during her visit last week, she told me I needed to bring him to you directly. He no longer comes when I call, he paces and walks in circles constantly, and worst of all"—she lowered her voice—"he can't seem to control his bodily functions. When he's not doing any of that, he sits and stares at nothing, unresponsive to me or anyone else."

On the verge of tears, Mrs. Danforth added, "Please, Miss, I lost my husband last year and my son a few years before that. He's all I've got left."

Sophia's heart broke for the poor woman, especially considering there was no hope to offer. Sophia had seen the dog's symptoms before and was fairly certain of the problem.

"How far have you traveled, Mrs. Danforth?"

"Not terribly far. I live in a small village three hours south of here. I probably should have sent a letter instead, but it might have taken weeks for your reply to reach me, and Mrs. Hilliard assured me you wouldn't mind if I came. I called first at Talford Hall, and your kind butler directed me here. I hope I am not intruding."

"Not at all," Sophia said. "I'm glad you have come. It sounds as though you have had a long journey, though. You must be famished. May I offer you some tea? I can summon one of the grooms to look after Captain while we talk."

"Can you help him?" she asked hopefully.

Sophia hated that she would soon dash those hopes, but she couldn't bring herself to do so just yet. "I may be able to help you understand the situation, but I need to ask you a few questions first. Ah, here's Jed now. He will look after Captain and see that no harm comes to him. Will you join me?"

Mrs. Danforth seemed reluctant to hand over the leash, but when Jed crouched down to pet the dog and the animal didn't bark or shrink away, she capitulated.

Sophia made small talk until tea had been served and Mrs. Danforth appeared more restored. Only then did Sophia set her cup aside and ask, "How old is Captain, exactly?"

"I . . ." The woman's brow furrowed. "I do not know. My husband brought him home after a voyage a few years back. Said we should call him Captain because someone in the family should have that rank." She smiled at the memory. "My husband was in the navy, you know. He desperately yearned to become captain one day, but he died before his dream came to fruition."

"I think the name suits your dog perfectly."

She smiled.

"Was he brought to you as a puppy?"

"Puppy?" Mrs. Danforth snickered. "No. My husband found him half starved on a beach somewhere. He came home on leave with the creature in tow, telling me a ship was no place for a dog. I think he knew how lonely I'd been since the passing of our son. He knew Captain would be good company for me, and so he has—such good company."

The more Sophia learned about this sweet woman, her many struggles, and her beloved dog, the more her heart hurt. If only the lifeline of animals was not so short.

"I'm sorry to be the one to tell you this, Mrs. Danforth, but I believe Captain is showing signs of advanced age." She paused to let the news sink in. "If I am right, his symptoms will only worsen over time. I'm afraid there is nothing I, or anyone else, can do for him other than to tell you to enjoy what time you have left."

The teacup rattled against the saucer as Mrs. Danforth set it on the table with shaking hands. "Are you certain?"

"As certain as I can be without knowing his age. Like people, the minds of animals can deteriorate as they grow old. I've seen those symptoms before, and there is no mending something like that. I'm dreadfully sorry."

Mrs. Danforth closed her eyes and shook her head. The muscles in her jaw tensed and fidgeted before she gave in to the emotion and dropped her face into her hands, sobbing.

Sophia pulled a handkerchief from a nearby drawer and sat beside the woman. She wasn't sure what to say or do, so she tucked the cloth in Mrs. Danforth's hand and gave it a squeeze.

Much to her surprise, Hugh and Knave popped their heads into the room, looking curious, confused, and slightly alarmed. Sophia waved them away, wanting to give the woman some privacy.

Eventually, Mrs. Danforth's sobs subsided, and she lifted her swollen, tear-stained face to Sophia. "Forgive me, Miss Gifford. I can't seem to control myself."

Sophia gave her hand another squeeze. "There is nothing to forgive. Take all the time you need to mourn, just don't forget that Captain is not gone yet. He may not be himself any longer, but he is still here. Treasure the moments you have left."

Mrs. Danforth dried her eyes, straightened her shoulders, and nodded. "I will go to him now."

She began to rise, but Sophia put her hand on the woman's knee. "I'm sure he is resting, which is something you should do as well. I will have a maid make up a bedchamber for—"

"Oh no, I could never impose."

"Nonsense, Mrs. Danforth. From this moment forward you are my guest."

"But this isn't your home!"

Sophia smiled. "No, but it is my sister's, and we are hosting this house party together. I'm at liberty to invite whomever I wish, and right now it is my wish to extend an invitation to you. Please stay at least one night, Mrs. Danforth. We are kindred spirits after all, both sharing a love of animals. I would very much like you to stay."

"But I've brought no gowns, no nightclothes, or anything else."

That did present a bit of a problem, since Sophia's gowns would be too short and large for the frail-looking woman. But Abby was about her size.

"Ah, here are my friends and sister now. Pru, Abby, and Catherine, I'd like you to meet Mrs. Danforth. She has just learned her dog isn't aging well, and has traveled three hours to see me. Do help me convince her to stay the night with us."

Prudence snuggled her own dog close. "You must definitely stay. I will not hear otherwise. Don't you agree, Scamp?"

The dog barked in response, but Mrs. Danforth still appeared hesitant. "If you're certain I will be no trouble. "

"No trouble at all. I will notify Cook that we'll have one more for dinner." She rang the bell.

"I can just take dinner in my room."

"You'll do no such thing," said Prudence. "A new face is precisely what our house party needs. Are you here alone?"

Sophia answered for the woman, saying kindly, "Her husband passed on last year."

"I'm sorry to hear that," said Prudence.

Mrs. Danforth twisted her hands in her lap. "I really would feel more comfortable in my room. I didn't anticipate staying and have nothing suitable to wear."

Before Sophia could say anything, Abby intervened. "You look to be about my size, Mrs. Danforth. I'm sure we can find something to bring out those beautiful brown eyes of yours. What do you think, Catherine? Will my peach silk suit her coloring?"

"Indeed," said Catherine. "Especially if she couples it with my brown lace shawl."

"Oh, yes. That *would* be perfect," said Abby.

A small smile touched Mrs. Danforth's lips, and Sophia wanted to hug her sister and friends for their acceptance of a stranger. How blessed she was to be surrounded by such good people.

A maid appeared at the door and curtsied. "You rang, milady?"

"Oh, yes. Thank you, Lily. Will you show Mrs. Danforth to the green room and tell Cook we'll have one or two more for dinner?" She smiled at their guest. "I'm assuming you'd like to get settled and perhaps enjoy a rest before dinner?"

"That sounds heavenly."

When Mrs. Danforth rose to follow the maid, Abby said, "Catherine and I will stop in a little before dinner with that gown. I'm sure my maid would love to arrange your hair as well."

"Thank you ever so much," said Mrs. Danforth. "I feel as though I've happened upon a house full of angels."

"We have our moments." Prudence nuzzled her dog's nose with her own. "But we can also be quite devious when we wish to be. Isn't that right, Scamp?"

Sophia laughed. "Lady Knave more so than the rest of us. Have a care, Mrs. Danforth, or you may unwittingly become a pawn in her next scheme."

Prudence scowled at her sister before waving a flippant hand at their guest. "Sophia likes to tease me is all. Now off you go, Mrs. Danforth. We shall see you at dinner."

As soon as she'd gone, Prudence passed Scamp to Catherine and summoned a passing footman. She quickly scribbled a note and handed it to him. "Will you take this to Mr. Hatherly immediately? Please convey my apologies for the short notice."

*Oh dear,* thought Sophia. Prudence was up to her matchmaking again. A middle-aged man on the outskirts of Lynfield, Mr. Hatherly had also lost a spouse. He had no idea about the surprise that would await him this evening, should he accept.

Sophia cocked her head. "You do realize Mrs. Danforth won't be in the most cheerful of moods. She's mourning her dog."

Abby poured herself some tea. "Perhaps Mr. Hatherly will be a distraction."

"My thoughts exactly," said Prudence. "The poor woman looked in desperate need of a diversion."

Sophia sighed, Abby sipped her tea, and Catherine laughed. "I suppose I should be grateful you have not attempted to match me with someone, Pru."

"Should I ever stumble across a man worthy of you, I would try. Sadly, the Calloway twins are the only eligible bachelors in the vicinity. You really must join us in London next year."

Sophia caught Catherine's eye and shook her head in what she thought was a covert manner.

"I saw that," scolded Prudence, pointing a finger at her sister. "Need I remind you that you wouldn't have found Mr. Fawcett had you not accompanied me to London?"

Sophia smoothed her skirts and nodded. "It's true. Catherine, should you find yourself in the market for a man, by all means, go with my sister. She will see that you are invited to every party and meet every eligible man in town. You will be badgered daily, pushed into uncomfortable situations, and made to feel as though you don't know your own mind."

"But not to worry," added Abby dryly. "Because she'll always have your best interests at heart. Unless her own interests supersede them, that is."

"I protest!" Prudence glared at her sister and friend while they laughed. She lifted her dog to face her. "They are ungrateful wretches, are they not?"

He barked and squirmed so Prudence set him back on her lap. "I hope Mrs. Danforth will be more appreciative."

"I'm sure she will," said Sophia with a smile.

# ELEVEN

AT DINNER THAT evening, Lord Dodious insisted on taking Sophia into dinner. Much to her chagrin, Hugh gracefully capitulated, offering his arm to Catherine instead. Sophia tried to hide her displeasure, but when Lord Dodious did his best to find fault with Mrs. Danforth, it became a sore trial.

"Are you certain she is who she claims to be?" he asked.

Sophia could only hope his voice hadn't carried to the other side of the table where Mrs. Danforth sat with Mr. Hatherly. "For goodness sake, Lord Do"—she cleared her throat—"Daglum, do you think she intends to run off with the silver?"

"Those of good breeding don't arrive at a stranger's door and insist on staying the night."

"It was Lady Knave who insisted she stay, not Mrs. Danforth."

"I seriously doubt that," he said in his patronizing way.

Sophia bit her tongue and looked down at her plate to hide her frustration. How she ached to be seated with Hugh and Catherine. Judging by their laughter, they were having a marvelous time.

As soon as dinner concluded, Sophia couldn't escape to the drawing room quickly enough. Her reprieve was short-lived, however, when the men arrived soon after. She tried to catch Hugh's eye, but it was Lord Dodious who spotted her first and moved to take the empty spot on the sofa at her side.

Desperate to avoid another painful conversation, she practically darted for Hugh.

"Would you care to take a stroll through the garden with me?" The words came out rushed and a little too loud. Several heads looked her way, including her mother and father's. Shocked and appalled, they appeared ready to throttle her.

Sophia felt her face grow warm, but she refused to apologize for her brazenness. Let her parents think what they wished. She did not care.

*Say something, Hugh,* she thought, staring at him.

He seemed to hesitate, then glanced in Lord Daglum's direction before finally saying, "I would love nothing more, Miss Gifford." He sounded so stiff and formal, as though he was being made to do something he'd rather not.

"Sophia, it is too cold for a walk outside," her mother said firmly.

"You can borrow my wrap." Prudence practically stuffed it into Sophia's hands. "This will keep you perfectly warm."

"Er . . . thank you." Hugh obviously didn't want to go with her, her mother stared daggers at her, and Prudence was practically pushing them out the door.

Perhaps Sophia had acted a bit too rashly.

"Would anyone else care to join us?" Hugh asked, no doubt realizing they would need a chaperone of some sort.

"Brigston and I could use some air," said Abby.

Her husband, who had been in mid-conversation with Knave, looked up in surprise. "We could? Oh. Yes, we could."

Sophia tried not to wince. How outrageously bold she must appear—asking a man to walk alone with her in the moonlit gardens without inviting any others to join them. What must everyone think of her? What must Hugh?

Why did she care?

Hugh helped her with the shawl, and by the time they finally left the awkwardness behind, Sophia wanted to sink into the ground and disappear.

Abby and Brigston trailed behind them for a time before wandering down a side path. Their voices grew softer and softer before disappearing altogether.

Sophia inhaled deeply and tried to forget about the scene she'd just made. It was a lovely evening despite the chill in the air. Stars sparkled in the sky high overhead and the nearly full moon glowed brightly. Her peaceful surroundings gradually calmed her, and she felt herself relax.

She clung a little tighter to Hugh's arm, welcoming the warmth of his body and the scent of sandalwood. How interesting that a smell that had seemed so ordinary all her life now took on a pleasurable, tantalizing quality.

"Forgive me, Hugh. I'm not sure what came over me. I just couldn't bear the thought of another moment in that man's company."

He slipped his free hand over hers briefly and gave it a squeeze. "I'm flattered you prefer my conversation to his. Or am I merely the lesser of two evils?"

"You know you are not." A light breeze tickled her neck, and she tugged the shawl higher for additional warmth.

"Are you cold?" He stopped walking to examine her.

She might have said yes if she thought he'd pull her close to keep her warm, but it was just wishful thinking. He'd probably suggest they go back inside. So she shook her head, thinking she'd have to be chilled to the bone before willingly returning to the drawing room.

"I'm perfectly content," she said.

"You're perfectly lovely too. That blue suits you."

His words took away some of the chill. "Do not put me to the blush, sir. My poor face is already too pink."

He chuckled and resumed walking. "Very well. Instead, I will tell you that you effectively thwarted Lord Daglum's plans to hold your attention captive the remainder of the evening. He even turned down my invitation for another game of cards, which happened to thwart *my* plans. 'Tis a shame, too, as I was feeling very lucky."

Under any other circumstances, his flirtatious grin would have weakened her knees and set her pulse awry, but she wasn't in the right mood.

She frowned and gazed down at the moonlit stone walkway. "You wished to play cards again?"

Her words came out flat, disappointed, but he mustn't have noticed because his tone remained teasing. "How else am I to recoup my losses from last night?"

His flippancy struck a nerve, and Sophia's jaw tightened. Did Hugh intend to strike up a game every night from here on out? Did he love gambling that much, or was he merely hoping her father would lose even more? She'd thought he'd come here to help, to find a way to save Talford, but that didn't seem to be the case any longer. Now he was merely aiding in its downfall.

She pulled her arm free and faced him. "I don't understand. Why would you organize another game when you know my father will play as well? He is not lucky, Hugh. He never has been. All he's ever done is lose, and we cannot afford to lose any more. You of all people should understand that."

"Sophie." He tried to take her hand, but she refused to let him, backing away from him instead. He watched her cautiously, then lifted his hands the way one might do when approaching a rabid animal.

"I *do* understand, Sophie." There was no hint of teasing in his voice now. "My apologies for making light of the situation."

When the back of her knees made contact with a bench, she slumped down, grabbing the seat with her hands. Perhaps she was being unfair. It shouldn't be Hugh's responsibility to save her family home or keep her father from the tables. It should be her father's.

She closed her eyes, wishing this entire evening away. "It is I who should apologize. My family's problems are not yours and never should be."

Silence followed her words, and she looked up to see him rubbing the back of his neck as though it ached. Moonlight darkened the lines in his face, making him appear older. Tired.

"Believe it or not, I did come to help," he said quietly. "My suggestion to play cards had nothing to do with—"

"Mr. Quinton," a voice hissed through the darkness. "You out 'ere?"

Hugh furrowed his brown and squinted. "Park? Is that you?"

"Aye." A tall, lanky man walked into the clearing wearing a footman's livery. Sophia recognized him from dinner. His red hair and ill-fitting uniform had made him hard to ignore.

Hugh sighed. "Have you come to lecture me about making you dress as a footman for no reason? Lord Daglum wasn't interested in a game of cards."

"Not surprised," said the man called Park.

"Why do you say that?"

"After dinner, 'e asked about the footman—the one I

replaced. Got all upset when I said 'e'd been relieved of 'is duties for the evenin'.'"

Hugh went silent for a moment before stating, "You think Lord Daglum had help at the tables."

"Aye. No other reason why 'e'd care about a footman."

Sophia listened in confusion to the exchange. As they continued to talk, however, understanding dawned.

She rose to her feet. "Are you saying Lord Daglum cheated?"

Park blinked at her in surprise, then shuffled his feet. "Pardon, Miss. Didn't realize we 'ad company."

She waved off his apology. "No matter. I am used to going unnoticed."

"I doubt that," he said. "Your hair's as orange as mine. Sort of 'ard to miss."

"Park," said Hugh in a warning voice.

The footman looked down at his shoes. "Pardon again, Miss. Didn't mean any offense."

Sophia smiled, liking his frank way of speaking. "No offense taken, Park, and you're right. My hair does draw notice, just not the sort I desire. Now back to the subject at hand. Do you truly believe Lord Daglum is a cheat?"

"One thing's for sure. 'E's a blubberin', brandy-faced b—"

"Park," Hugh warned again.

The footman looked sheepishly at Sophia, but when he saw her trying not to smile, he grinned.

Hugh cleared his throat. "Any chance you can question the footman you replaced and encourage him to talk?"

Park's grin widened. "Oh, 'e'll talk all right. Just leave it to me."

Hugh nodded, and Park disappeared as quickly and silently as he'd come.

Sophia watched him leave, a little concerned. The man had been giddy at the idea of "encouraging" someone to talk. "What will he do to the footman, do you think?"

Hugh chuckled. "Park isn't one to engage in fisticuffs—he's not built for it. But he is clever and cunning and has his own way of getting information. Although he never talks about his past, I'm fairly certain he was once a spy."

"I see." Sophia turned to find Hugh staring down at her, his expression one she could not read. She swallowed. "That's the reason you challenged Lord Daglum to a game of cards, isn't it?"

He continued peering at her through the darkness. "I'm no gambler, Sophie. I've made it to where I am because of hard work and learning to use my head, not because I'm lucky at the tables."

She swallowed again and closed her eyes. "You must think me a complete wretch."

He lifted her chin with his finger, encouraging her to look at him. He smiled, and his dimple appeared. "A beautiful wretch."

There was that slight burr again, charming and iresistible. Her heart tripped and stuttered at his nearness. His intoxicating scent assailed her, along with another, lighter aroma. How badly she wanted to step into his arms and press her lips to his. Kissing him couldn't be anything less than sublime.

His gaze actually dropped to her mouth for one brief moment before falling away. He took a few steps back, breaking the connection between them.

"Forgive me, Sophie."

She tried to smile, but she probably looked more sad than happy. "For what? Calling me a wretch?"

"Er . . . yes."

Sophia didn't believe him, and she desperately wanted the moment back. "You *should* be sorry. You are supposed to be courting me, and calling me a wretch is not a gentlemanly way to go about it. Come to think of it, you've been doing a poor job of it lately."

"Of what? Calling you a wretch?"

"No. *Courting* me," she clarified.

His lips quirked, and his eyes crinkled with suppressed humor. "Have I?"

"Yes." Sophia could scarce believe her boldness, but she had a very real fear that if she didn't say or do something to keep him at Radbourne, he would find a reason to leave. She wasn't ready for that.

"You've accompanied me on only one morning ride, you proposed a game of cards over pandering to my every whim—although to be fair I cannot hold that against you any longer—and this evening you allowed Lord Dodious to take me into dinner even though I detest the man. To add insult to injury, here we are alone in a moonlit garden, which I had to orchestrate, mind you, and you don't even *try* to kiss me. Honestly, Hugh, I expected more from you."

Oh my, had she truly just said that? If her mother could hear her now, she'd take Sophia by the ear and drag her from the house.

Moonlight sparkled in Hugh's eyes, and his mouth quirked into a smile. He took one slow step forward, then another. The smell of sandalwood and vanilla invaded her senses, and a breeze lifted the stray curls on her neck. She shivered, but not because she felt cold.

He dropped his voice to a murmur. "I thought this was a feigned courtship, for the eyes of your parents and the benefit of Mr. Fawcett."

"It is," she said.

"Your parents are not here now."

"No," she breathed. "But you cannot kiss me in their presence without compromising me. Isn't it better to return me looking like I've been thoroughly kissed and let them wonder?"

He chuckled. "Now you want a thorough job of it, do you? Are you hoping your father—or worse, Lord Daglum—will challenge me to a duel?"

She brightened. "Could you beat him? Lord Daglum, I mean."

"No."

"Drat."

He snickered, but she was a far cry from doing the same. Instead, her heart wilted. She'd practically begged him to kiss her, and not only had he found a way to change the subject, he was now laughing at her.

Another breeze floated by, and this time she shivered because of the cold. "I suppose we should return before my mother comes looking for us." She turned to go, but he stopped her with a hand on her shoulder.

"Sophie, it isn't that I—"

"There you are," said Abby through the darkness. "I was beginning to think you'd gone back inside and left us to weather the cold on our own."

Hugh's hand dropped to his side, taking what little warmth she'd felt with it.

As Abby stepped into the clearing, Sophia immediately noticed the glow. Abby's cheeks were slightly red, her lips swollen, and her hair a little less perfect than it had been before.

*At least one of us got a thorough kissing*, Sophia thought. She tried not to be jealous of her friend, but the pangs came nonetheless.

"We were just about to go in," said Sophia.

"Lead on," said Abby. "We thought another game of charades would be just the thing."

Sophia couldn't do it. She couldn't smile or laugh or even pretend to have fun. What she wanted to do most was curl into a ball and cry.

"You'll have to play without me," she said. "Lord Daglum has given me an abominable headache, and I wish to retire."

Abby's forehead furrowed, and she seemed to finally realize that Sophia wasn't in the same state of bliss. "I'm sorry to hear that. Would you like me to go with you to your room?"

Sophia shook her head. "What I would like is for you to enjoy the remainder of the evening with the others. I shall be good as new tomorrow."

That was probably a lie. Sophia had a feeling she would never be as good as new again, at least not until this wretched house party had concluded. If only she could snap her fingers and begin the evening anew. How different she'd go about it.

When they neared the house, Sophia allowed Brigston and Abby to precede her inside. She and Hugh followed in their shadows, but as soon as the opportunity arose, she slipped away to her bedchamber.

As penance for her earlier lie, an ache began throbbing in her head as she prepared for bed.

# TWELVE

Sophia was fluffing her pillow, attempting to find a comfortable position, when her door flew open. Backlit by the candlelight flickering in the hallway, her mother's angry stance made Sophia wish she'd already fallen asleep.

"Sophia Eleanor Gifford, what on earth were you thinking, throwing yourself at that . . . that man?"

Sophia groaned and rolled to the side. "I wasn't throwing myself at Hugh, Mother. I was trying to avoid Lord Dodious."

Her mother didn't seem to notice the disparaging nickname. Instead, she traipsed to Sophia's bedside table and lit the candle. The small flame highlighted the frustrated lines on her mother's face. "Mr. Quinton is a man undeserving of your notice, yet you call him by his Christian name?"

Sophia gave up on sleep and rolled onto her back. Her head still throbbed, and her body had never felt more weary. Could this conversation not wait until morning? From the look in her mother's eye, it could not—or rather, *would* not.

"I have called him Hugh as long as I can remember, and I will continue doing so. He is my friend, and I address my friends in a less formal manner." Shadows danced across her ceiling, and branches scraped against the large window. The earlier breeze had turned into a strong wind.

"Do you mean to tell me he calls you Sophia?"

The reckless feeling that had begun earlier still raged inside Sophia. Perhaps she was tired of being her mother's pawn or perhaps she was beginning to go mad. Either way, she did not choose her words carefully.

"Of course not. I am Sophie to him."

Her mother's mouth fell open, and her cheeks turned an angry pink. "How could you allow such familiarity? Not even Mr. Fawcett or Lord Daglum use your Christian name."

"Only because the subject has never come up with Mr. Fawcett, and I would rather move to the West Indies than hear my name on the lips of that pompous, horrible Lord Dodious."

Quiet ensued, something that didn't often occur with her mother. After a time, her shoulders sagged, and the anger seemed to seep out of her.

She slowly sank down on the edge of the bed. "You despise him that much?"

"I loathe him." Sophia debated telling her mother about the cheating, only to dismiss the idea. Although it would serve in her favor, the news would undoubtedly reach her father, and there was no telling how he'd react. It was best to let Hugh handle the situation.

Her mother sighed, looking down at her hands. "What is the point of being a mother if one's daughters refuse to listen?"

Sophia managed a small smile. "I always listen, Mother. I just don't always agree."

"You *rarely* agree." Her mother slowly removed her white lace gloves, one finger at a time, then clenched her fingers around it.

"I don't wish misery upon you, you know."

"I should hope not."

The corners of her mother's mouth moved in the general direction of a smile, but the sadness in her eyes seemed to weigh them back down.

"Sophia, I don't think you understand what it's like to be at the bottom of one's class. Mr. Gifford is a respectable man, but so many doors were closed to us, so many opportunities. I can't tell you how many times I have felt the humiliation of being looked down upon. I don't wish the same for you."

Her mother twisted her gloves around her fingers. "Lord Daglum has his faults, to be sure, but as his wife, every door will be open to you. You will be a marchioness, Sophie—a person to be revered."

Sophia pushed her bedclothes back and scooted forward. She gently removed the gloves from her mother's grasp before they became too ruined.

"Perhaps I would be invited to more balls and events, but you know as well as I that there are still plenty of people who would find reasons to look down on me. If I don't dress in the perfect stare of fashion, if I do the unthinkable and go out into the sun without a bonnet, if I say the wrong thing or behave in a way unbefitting a marchioness—heavens, my freckles and red hair are reason enough! I am what I am, Mother, and I would prefer to marry a man I care for and respect than one I cannot."

Her mother inhaled deeply and exhaled slowly. "Very well. I will cease my matchmaking efforts with Lord Daglum." Sophia nearly squealed in delight until her mother added, "But you must promise me one thing."

"What?"

"Promise me you will choose Mr. Fawcett over Mr. Quinton."

A lump formed in Sophia's throat. It should be an easy

promise to make. After all, it was one thing to marry an untitled gentleman with little means, another to wed a man her family could not invite to a London ball. Still, Sophia hesitated in her answer for reasons she couldn't explain. Wasn't this exactly what she'd been hoping for? The reason she'd invited Mr. Fawcett to the house party? The reason Hugh had begun to "court" her?

She should be ecstatic.

Their plan had worked.

Sophia swallowed the lump and nodded. "I promise."

A look of relief settled across her mother's features, and she reached out to touch Sophia's arm in a rare moment of tenderness. "Thank you, my dear. Thank you."

Sophia should have been pleased. She should have felt the same sense of relief. But the only feeling that came over her was one of discontent, as though she'd said something very, very wrong.

# THIRTEEN

HUGH STEPPED INTO the breakfast parlor and immediately searched the room for Sophie. She wasn't there. He should have expected as much.

Lady Knave, who had just filled her plate, stopped beside him and lowered her voice. "Sophia could no more bring herself to watch a pheasant fall from the sky than she could a person. She will not be joining our excursion this morning. She has chosen to finish the invitations for our soirée next week instead."

Hugh considered feigning confusion, as if he'd been searching the room for Lord Knave and not Sophia, but Lady Knave would undoubtedly see through that farce. He smiled ruefully instead. "I figured as much, but it never hurts to hope."

She smiled. "I like you, Mr. Quinton. I hope you don't intend to go away anytime soon."

He wasn't sure what she meant by that, but he appreciated her kind words. In fact, he appreciated all the kindness that had been extended to him. Sophie's sister and small circle of friends were . . . different. From the beginning, they'd welcomed Hugh and made him feel as though he belonged. Sometimes, he even found himself thinking he could.

Then he'd come back to reality and remember he was only a tadpole in a pond of exotic fish.

Which begged the question: What was he still doing here? He'd discovered nothing to save Talford, at least not without a significant investment on Mr. Gifford's part. And Sophie—well, she was not for him. However much he wished it could be otherwise, she was out of his reach, to say nothing of her understanding with Mr. Fawcett.

"I wouldn't have taken you for a hunter," said a voice that caused the hair on Hugh's arms to bristle.

He cocked his head at Lord Daglum and shrugged. "I have many interests."

In truth, Hugh had purchased the shotgun only a fortnight prior. Park had given him a few tutorials on how the gun worked, but Hugh had yet to actually shoot the thing. Hunting was something the upper class did for sport, and he'd never had the time for that particular pursuit. A morning ride, a good book, or a harmless game of cards now and again were the extent of his leisurely activities.

If Hugh had learned one thing since coming to this house party, too much leisure was not to his liking. Talford Hall had initially kept him occupied, but that wasn't the case any longer. Other than hoping for a miracle to save the estate—a fruitless endeavor—he had nothing to do. There was little satisfaction in wandering the grounds or doing nothing in particular.

Yet another reason why he and Sophie would never suit. She seemed to enjoy the life she led, whereas he didn't care for it at all. The only thing he was coming to care for was her.

Dangerous territory.

Hugh filled a plate and sat with the others, but his mind continued to roam elsewhere. At some point, Mr. and Mrs. Gifford arrived, but they didn't even spare him a glance.

After loading into carriages, the group was transported to grassy fields where servants held back the hounds who would soon prod the pheasants into flight. It was a well organized affair, but even if Hugh managed to hit a bird, the sense of accomplishment would be palled with the knowledge that the birds had been stocked on the land for the sole purpose of being hunted.

"You don't know your way around a shotgun, do you?" Lord Daglum sneered, obviously noticing Hugh's lack of experience.

"Never had a use for one before today."

The other man chuckled, his tone disparaging. "No, I gather not."

Hugh chose to think of it as a compliment. There was nothing wrong with choosing more worthwhile pursuits, especially considering cheating wasn't among them.

"Allow me to demonstrate how it is done," said Lord Daglum. He tapped his foot impatiently as he waited for the others to take their places. The men were lined up in a neat little row, while the women chatted and watched from behind.

Lord Knave eventually signaled to the servants that all was ready, and the hounds were released. The dogs raced through the meadow, barking and yapping, and a host of pheasants took flight. Shots rang out, birds fell, and the ladies cheered as Hugh slowly lowered his gun.

Deuce take it, he hadn't even had time to aim before it was all over.

Perhaps he should have practiced a little.

As the morning dragged on, the dogs continued to stir birds into flight, but after the initial wave, fewer targets remained. If Hugh had hoped to shoot one, he should have done it in the beginning.

He was reloading his gun when a sorry looking mutt darted into the clearing. Filthy and scrawny, it clenched its jaws around a lifeless bird. The servants and hounds began racing after the poor dog, who was now running in the direction of Hugh and Lord Daglum, unwilling to give up its lunch.

Amused, Hugh watched it outrun the other dogs, quietly cheering it on. Lord Daglum had other ideas. Instead of allowing the mutt to run free, he ran to intercept it, kicking it hard as it passed. The dog let out a cry, dropped the bird, and landed in an unmoving heap not far from Hugh's boots.

"Worthless mongrel," muttered Lord Daglum as he stalked towards the dog, looking like he meant to kick it again.

Hugh stepped forward and let the barrel of his gun fall to the ground between Lord Daglum and the dog, causing Lord Daglum to kick the gun instead.

"What the devil are you doing?" he growled.

"What are you?" Hugh challenged. "This dog has done you no harm."

"No harm?" Lord Daglum scoffed. "That *dog*, if it can be called such, is poaching our dinner."

The others gathered around as Hugh crouched down to feel if the animal still breathed. Although faint, he could feel its belly rise and fall.

"Is it alive?" Prudence asked quietly.

"Yes."

Much to his surprise, Mrs. Gifford bent down and softly touched the dog's head with her gloved finger. She lifted it to find a smudge of blood.

"You must take this poor creature to Sophia straightaway. She'll know what to do." She stood and looked sternly at Lord Daglum, allowing her expression to convey her displeasure.

He had the decency to appear abashed. Good. Perhaps next time he'd think twice before treating another animal in a similar fashion.

Hugh carefully scooped up the dog and cradled it against his chest. It felt frail and lifeless. He climbed into the nearest carriage and asked the coachman to return him to Radbourne with all possible speed. Fifteen minutes later, he stood in the stables, stroking the dog as he waited impatiently for Sophia to be summoned.

The coachman briefly inspected the animal before shaking his head. "Looks bad, sir. You sure you want Miss Gifford seein' that? It might never wake up."

Hugh had to concede the man was right. Limp, with blood matting its hair, the dog appeared dead already. But his scrawny stomach still moved, and Sophie would never forgive him if he let the animal die without trying to save it. She was made of sterner stuff than most women. Together, they could give this creature a chance.

"Fetch me some clean water, cloths, and a blanket. Miss Gifford will be here shortly," said Hugh.

Before the coachman could even take a step, Sophie rushed into the stables, looking frantic. Park and Mrs. Danforth were not far behind.

Sophie barely glanced at Hugh before dropping to her knees. She inspected the dog for a moment, then scooped it up, not caring about the dirt or blood staining her pretty blue dress.

"Tell me what happened," she said to Hugh as they strode towards the house.

"He was kicked in the head."

"On purpose?"

"Yes."

Her jaw clenched, but she didn't ask for more details. "Mrs. Danforth? Park? Do either of you have any medical knowledge, or should I send for a doctor?"

"Aye, Miss," said Park. "I can stitch up the wound."

Mrs. Danforth was dressed in the same traveling gown she had worn the day before—obviously ready to leave—but that didn't stop her from adding, "I can help as well. I have nursed my husband for various injuries."

"Good," said Sophie. "Let us take the poor thing to the kitchen and doctor it there. I shall have a maid find a basket for a bed. With any luck, we shall see it through this."

Hugh's steps slowed as he allowed Sophie to precede him into the house. In all his years and associations, he'd never met a better person than she. The dog couldn't have landed in more caring hands.

Mrs. Danforth and Park fussed over the creature until it had been cleaned and stitched. Although much too thin, once its mangy hair had been washed, the dog no longer looked half dead. Double the size of Scamp, and coated in gray and white fur, it actually appeared charming in a wild sort of way.

At some point, the dog regained consciousness and began whimpering and squirming, but Sophie's soothing words and soft touch calmed it right down. She fed it water and some scraps before gently moving it to the large basket a maid had kindly made into a bed.

Mrs. Danforth peered down at the dog with fondness. "What should we call him?"

"I have no idea," said Sophia. "I have never been good with names. Do you have a suggestion?"

"What about . . ." Mrs. Danforth paused as she lightly stroked the dog's belly. "Commander." It was the rank of a naval officer just below captain.

It wouldn't have been Hugh's first choice of a name, especially for a dog of such small stature, but apparently Sophia thought differently.

"It's perfect," she said.

Park appeared more skeptical. He scratched his head, leaving a lock of red hair sticking out. "'Appen you'll call him Com or . . . Mand?" He frowned at his own suggestions, and Hugh snickered.

Park had never liked long names. He'd as lief call Hugh "sir" rather than Mr. Quinton, but shortening Commander wasn't an easy task.

Mrs. Danforth gave Park an odd look. "Only think how confusing that would be. When you call for the poor creature, would you say, 'Come, Com' or 'Come, Mand'? Hardly. No, Commander will suit him just fine."

From the look on Park's face he didn't agree, but at least he kept his opinion to himself.

"I wonder, Mrs. Danforth," said Sophia slowly. "Would you consider staying an additional night? I had thought to keep Commander in my bedchamber with me, but it might be wiser to place him under your expert care—at least until he is out of the woods."

The woman didn't hesitate. Her small frame straightened, and a look of confidence lit up her features. "I would be happy to be of assistance, Miss Gifford. Shall I take him up now and get him settled?"

"You are a dear," said Sophia. "Park, would you—" She didn't have to finish the sentence. Park had already picked up the basket and was gesturing for Mrs. Danforth to show him the way.

As his lanky legs followed the woman's frail body from the room, Hugh overheard Park say, "What about callin' it Mate instead? Seems a mite easier on the tongue."

"I still prefer Commander," insisted Mrs. Danforth.

Hugh didn't bother to hide his grin, and when his gaze met Sophie's, they shared a quiet laugh. He couldn't resist elbowing her in a conspiratorial way. "Me thinks you are up to something, Miss Gifford."

"Indeed I am. As much as I detest Lord Dodious for harming that dog, something good may come from it. Won't Commander make an excellent second in command to Captain?"

"And perhaps become a source of comfort to Mrs. Danforth when the greyhound passes on?"

"My thoughts exactly." She faced him, and her grin softened into an expression that made Hugh's heart lurch. "Thank you for saving it."

"I was only the delivery boy."

She touched his arm and shook her head. "You are more than that."

The warmth of her hand, mingled with the spark in her gaze, sent a wave of desire through Hugh. He should have said, "'Twas nothing," and found a reason to leave, but he didn't want to. He craved more time—more of this, more of her.

"Would you care to take a stroll through the woods with me, Sophie? For old times' sake?"

"I'd love nothing more."

She slipped her arm through his, smiled up at him, and Hugh wondered how he'd ever return to London alone.

# FOURTEEN

"I'VE BEEN THINKING about Talford, Sophie," said Hugh as they sauntered beyond the gardens towards the woods that separated the two estates. It was in those woods they'd once caught lizards and spent hours talking, scheming, and laughing. He missed those days, when their only care had been how to evade their parents and her governess.

"Do we have to talk about that now?" she asked, a plea in her voice.

Hugh smiled and pointed to a large oak that towered above the surrounding trees in the distance. "Do you remember that tree? It had the perfect branch for that swing we never got to build."

"You remember."

"How could I forget? You talked of nothing else every time we passed it—how you wanted to find a thick wooden plank for the seat and carve out holes for the ropes. You made it sound like a simple task to scale a thirty-foot tree and tie knots around that precarious looking branch."

She chuckled. "I used to think you could do anything. I still do."

Hugh knew she hadn't meant to pressure him, but he still felt the weight of Talford bear down on him. She may not want to talk about it, but there were a few things they needed to discuss.

"I can't do everything, Sophie. I can't find a way to make your home self-sustaining again. Things are going to have to change, whether you want them to or not."

She sighed, and to his surprise, she seemed more resigned than upset. "I know."

"You could charge a fee for your help with animals," he suggested feebly, knowing she would have to help a lot of animals and charge a hefty sum.

She shook her head. "I could never ask for payment."

*That is the difference between your world and mine,* Hugh thought. He had no problem requiring a fee for his services. It might make him a tradesman, but it also allowed him to live a comfortable life.

The upper class may not want to admit it, but they, too, accepted payments in the form of rents and revenues from crops, cattle, and other things. Why that was an acceptable form of work had never made sense to Hugh. It was not an easy feat to successfully manage an estate. It required a man to be fully involved in all aspects. Those who left that work to the hands of others were those who eventually had to seek the help of someone like Hugh.

"There are worse things than sullying one's hands in trade," Hugh finally said.

"You misunderstand." She slowed her pace to pick her way through a rocky area. "My feelings have nothing to do with societal expectations and everything to do with the fact that most of the people who come to me for help can't afford to pay me. Take Mrs. Danforth, for example. It is obvious she hasn't purchased a new gown in ages because she hasn't the means to do so. She merely loves her dog and was desperate for a way to help him. I would feel like a beast if I charged her a fee."

When Sophie put it that way, Hugh had to agree. So much for that idea, however fledgling it had been.

"Sophie, I don't know what else—"

She spun around to face him. "If I were to marry, would my dowry help matters?"

Hugh frowned, not liking the question. He didn't want Sophie to marry for the sake of saving her estate. He didn't want her to marry at all.

Unless . . .

No. He couldn't even contemplate that. Two different people. Two different worlds.

"Your dowry would become your husband's," he said.

"I know. But if I were to marry a kind man who agreed to use some of it to help Talford—"

"It would take more than some, Sophie, and even then, you would just be prolonging the inevitable. I would rather see you—or rather, your husband—invest the money more wisely."

"Couldn't we use it to build new tenant farms?"

"Where?"

She shrugged. "I don't know. Talford isn't the largest of estates, I realize, but surely some of our unused land could be turned into additional farms."

"I've already looked into that, but what land you have left isn't fit for farming—at least not without taking extensive and costly measures. You are surrounded by wetlands. The drainage alone would be nearly insurmountable."

"What about investing in land elsewhere?"

Hugh furrowed his brow. "Do you mean to sell Talford and purchase another estate?"

"No. I'm sure that isn't an option either, considering Talford couldn't possibly be worth much as things stand right now. I meant other land—you know, other *unused* land." She frowned at her own suggestion and sagged her shoulders in defeat. "It's no use, is it? We're going to have to sell."

He nodded solemnly. "I'm sorry, Sophie."

She pressed her lips together before asking, "Will we be able to afford a small cottage?"

Hugh didn't answer right away. There was another option—one he didn't relish mentioning because of what it meant for him. But this was Sophie. More than anything, he wanted her to be comfortably settled and happy.

"If you intend to marry, Sophie, you'll likely not need a cottage. You will have a home with your husband, and your parents with either you or your sister."

She bit her lower lip, and her throat constricted as she swallowed. "If I don't marry? Is a small cottage within the realm of possibilities?"

"A modest dwelling in the country, yes."

"Somewhere close by?"

"I could look into it, if you'd like. See what's available."

She shook her head. "You've done more than enough, Hugh. I am only asking for information. I want to understand all of my options before moving forward with anything."

Hugh knew this couldn't be an easy time for her—dealing with a change in one's circumstances never was—but she exuded strength, as though ready to face whatever came her way with a stiff upper lip. He found it admirable, not to mention appealing. He wanted to pull her close and tell her she had nothing to worry about. He'd take care of things. He'd take care of her.

If only he was in a position to make such an offer.

"Sophie, I wish the circumstances were different. I wish . . ." He stopped, knowing he wasn't talking about

Talford any longer. Could she see it in his eyes? The desire. The frustration that their lives ran parallel to each other, with social customs dictating they should never intersect. What would she say if he asked her to give up her station and marry him? Would she consider it? Would she consider *him*?

He would never know because he would never ask.

"You wish what, Hugh?" she pressed, looking as though she wanted him to say something in particular—a line from some script in her mind, no doubt.

Unfortunately, he was no mind reader. "I wish I could have made you that swing," he said.

She smiled sadly. "Even if you had, I would have never let you risk your neck by climbing that tree."

He quirked a brow in mock offense. "You doubt my climbing prowess?"

She opened her mouth as if to deny the charge, then seem to think better of it and shrugged. "You did insist you could take on a highwayman at age fourteen."

"And so I could have."

She tsk-ed and shook her head. "Boys and their silly bravado. It's a good thing girls have more sense."

He chortled. "Says the girl who wanted to build a boat and ride it down the Thames."

"That was only wishful thinking as you well knew. Neither of us had the skills to craft a boat."

"Your faith in me is astounding," he said dryly.

Sophie's lips twitched once or twice, then she pressed her palm against her mouth to stifle her giggles. *Such a charming sound,* he thought. *Such a charming sight.*

Her nose and cheeks had begun to shed the burned skin, and a few additional freckles could be seen in places he hadn't noticed before, but she still looked fetching. Her eyes sparkled with mirth, her collar bone shook with laughter, and the shade of emerald she wore painted her eyes a vivid green. Add to that her alluring curves, and Hugh wondered how anyone didn't see her as a great beauty.

She continued to giggle, grasping his arm with one hand and her belly with another. "Oh, Hugh. How you make me laugh."

"At least I'm adept at something."

She threaded her arm through his once more, tugging him towards the trees. "Come. Let us escape into the woods before we are spotted and Mother sends for me."

Feeling lighthearted and impulsive all of a sudden, he let her pull him forward. "You'd think we were children again, doing our best to evade our parents."

"Let's pretend that we are and do something daring, like capture a snake. We can leave it under Lord D's pillow."

He chuckled. "A frog would fit nicely in his boot as well."

"Frogs need water," she said.

"We can add that too." Her charming giggle sounded again, and Hugh smiled.

They crossed the stream, tiptoeing over rocks, and eventually found the old tree stump where they'd carved their initials.

*Here sat SG and HQ,* it read.

Sophie pointed to the space above their initials. "We should add 'The Illustrious and Estimable' right there."

Hugh shook his head. "You obviously don't remember how long it took us to carve that much. I propose 'The Great' instead."

"Now you're beginning to sound like Park."

He took her by the waist and lifted her to the top of the stump. Even with the added height, she was only a few inches taller. "Don't ever tell him, or it'll go straight to his head. And gads, you're short."

"Petite," she said, resting her hands on his shoulders. "I prefer the word petite."

"Weren't we about the same height once?"

"You have certainly grown at least a head or two taller in the past decade. Perhaps all that youthful bravado had something to do with it."

He chuckled. Her waist was soft and perfectly curved. He wanted to pull her to him and feel more of her. Sample her lips. Smell the familiar scent of lavender in her hair.

"Sophie, I—" He clamped his mouth shut, cutting off what he'd been about to say. *I adore you.* Devil take it, who did he think he was? He had no right to hold her in this manner, alone in the woods. Only a cad would take such liberties.

"You what?" Her eyes probed his. *Say what I want you to say,* they seemed to plead.

"I think I prefer it when you are shorter than me." He swung her back to the ground. "Yes, that's better. When it comes to you, I need every advantage I can get."

She looked perplexed and even a little disappointed. "I have no idea what you mean by that."

Hugh forced himself to release her. "It means you are superior to me in every other way. You're kinder and more graceful. You also ride better and are far more beautiful and intelligent." *Not to mention a gentlewoman,* he added to himself. "You have me thoroughly bested, with the exception of height. I will always be taller."

"That is completely untrue."

"No, it isn't. Ask anyone. I *am* taller."

She laughed. "I wasn't referring to that, as you well know. Who saved that poor dog from Lord D's boot? Who saved me from being humiliated by my subpar musical talent? Who has saved many estates from ruin? Who came all this way to help an old friend? Who offered a young highwayman a better life? No one can hold a candle to you, Hugh Quinton, least of all me. Though I will admit, I *could* best you in a horse race."

"You also look better in gowns."

She grinned. "I should hope so."

He returned her grin and, heaven help him, took her hand. "Let's call a truce and say we are both superior creatures."

"Here, here," she agreed. "But are we superior enough to locate a snake?"

"And a frog," he reminded her. Then he snickered. "Perhaps we are not as kind as we'd like to think."

"On the contrary, sir. We will be doing everyone else a great kindness by finding a way to be rid of that man."

"Just leave it to me, Sophie. I have a plan."

She placed her free hand over her heart in a dramatic fashion. "You are my knight in shining armor, Sir Hugh."

"Indeed I am," he said with forced brightness, knowing that with her, he could never be anything more than an old childhood friend.

SOPHIE CREPT UP the back stairs, holding muddy boots and grinning at Hugh's parting words.

"Until later, my illustrious and estimable Sophie." Her heart trilled every time she recounted the scene in her mind. His bow, the feel of his lips on her hand as he kissed it, the teasing sparkle in his eyes. And oh, that smile.

There was no denying it any longer. She was head over heels in love with Hugh Quinton.

Sophia wanted to shout it out loud. Hang the social

customs, the expectations, the consequences. Hang her promise to her mother. Hang everything.

She peeked in on Mrs. Danforth and dropped her boots to the ground when she spotted the woman relaxing in a chair next to a sleeping Commander. Sophia crept inside, crouching low over the dog.

"How's he doing?" she asked.

"He whimpers every now and again, but I only have to rub his back and he calms right down."

*Yes, the two of them will get along just fine,* Sophia thought in satisfaction. She rose and perched on a wooden bench at the foot of the bed, tucking her bootless feet beneath her skirts. "How are *you,* Mrs. Danforth?"

The woman sighed and laid her head against the back of her chair with a contented smile. "If only I had known my little outing would turn into an adventure. I would have packed some clothes."

"I'm certain Abby can find another dress for you to borrow this evening," Sophia assured her.

"If it's all right with you, I'll take my dinner in my room this evening. I don't want to leave Commander alone."

"We can have a maid sit with Commander," said Sophia, "and I'm sure Prudence would happily invite Mr. Hatherly to dine with us again, if that is your wish."

Mrs. Danforth colored a bit then shook her head. "He is a kind man, but he doesn't care for dogs at all, and well . . . that will never do."

Sophia had to smile at that. "No, it definitely won't. I'm sorry if we made you uncomfortable."

"You didn't in the least," said Mrs. Danforth. "Mr. Hatherly was good natured, and I was able to set aside my troubles for a few hours. It would have been worse for me to keep to my room."

"Will it be worse for you to keep to your room tonight?" Sophia asked. "Should I insist that you dine with us?"

"No. I am better now. Commander has given me a reason not to wallow in self-pity any longer." She peered down at the dog with fondness.

Sophia leaned forward and touched the woman's arm. "Mrs. Danforth, I hate to ask anything more from you, but would you consider keeping Commander? I think that you are exactly what he needs."

Mrs. Danforth didn't say anything for a time, but when she finally looked up from the dog, tears shone in her eyes. "I was hoping you'd let me take him home. Thank you, Miss Gifford. For everything."

"You are welcome to stay as long as you'd like."

Mrs. Danforth gave Sophia's hand a squeeze. "I appreciate that, but unless Commander takes a turn for the worse, we will take our leave in the morning. It is time I go home."

Sophia nodded in understanding, then stood and walked to the door, pausing to say, "I am glad you made the journey here, Mrs. Danforth. It was a pleasure meeting you."

"And you, my dear."

Sophia collected her boots and continued down the hall, only to pause outside Abby's bedchamber when she heard her sister's laughter. She listened for a moment to be certain it was only Abby and Pru on the other side of the door before cracking it open and slipping inside. She found them curled up on Abby's bed, enjoying a cozy chat. Little Anne played with Scamp between them.

"You dare have a *tête-à-tête* without me?" Sophia asked, dropping her boots near the door before joining them on the bed. She kissed Anne on the forehead and ruffled Scamp's fur. "What have I missed?"

"Dog," said Anne, pointing to Scamp.

"How smart you are." Sophia smiled. "Do you know his name?"

"Dog," she said again, making them all laugh.

Prudence shifted positions to give Sophia more room. "We were merely trying to come up with the right word to describe Lord Daglum's callousness. Lord Braglum or Lord Bedlam are too tame. Abby suggested the insufferable Lord Dagabond—from vagabond, of course."

"Very fitting," Sophia agreed. "I've been thinking of him as Lord Dodious, but Lord Dagabond suits him as well." It was good Abby and Prudence were enjoying a laugh. If they'd been in the midst of a serious discussion, Sophia's uncontrollable grin would have drawn attention.

"I still don't think either name does him justice," said Prudence.

"Let's just say he is all that is vulgar and leave it at that," said Sophia. "Besides, if Hugh has his way, Lord D won't be around much longer."

They both brightened, but it was Abby who spoke first. "Mr. Quinton knows of a way to be rid of him? Do tell."

Sophia opened a book near Anne and began pointing at the pictures. "He discovered Lord D cheated at cards the other night and intends to confront him about it this afternoon. He's speaking with Knave and Brigston now."

"Truly?" Prudence clapped her hands in delight. "Oh, how I'd love to be a book on the shelf during that confrontation. Only think how cheerful tonight's dinner will be without Lord Dagabond in attendance. How perfectly wonderful. This day has just taken a turn for the better."

"Agreed," said Sophia, thinking of the blissful few hours she'd spent with Hugh in the woods. They never did find a snake or a frog, but it didn't matter. The fun had been in the search.

Sophia caught her sister watching her and quickly wiped the smile from her face.

"Speaking of turns for the better," said Abby, her fingers plucking at the embroidery on her pillow. "There is something I've been meaning to tell you both."

"Oh?" Prudence straightened, tucking her legs beneath her. "Have you and Brigston decided to purchase a home in Oxfordshire so you can live closer to us? Because that would be fabulous."

Abby laughed. "My news is even better than that, if you can imagine." She placed her hand on her stomach and said, almost shyly, "I'm increasing."

Sophia squealed and hugged her friend, but after glancing at her sister, she quickly sobered. Though Prudence tried to hide it behind a smile, the pain was there, plain as day.

She must have realized she'd been too transparent because she blurted, "I'm happy for you, Abby. Truly, I am." Her trembling voice belied her words.

"Oh, Pru," said Abby. "I'm so sorry. I shouldn't have said anything. I should have realized you—"

"Don't be silly," said Prudence as she wiped a few tears from her eyes. "I would have been extremely cross had you kept this from us. My tears have nothing to do with you and everything to do with the fact that I . . . I think something may be wrong with me."

Sophia wasn't entirely surprised, but having it out it the open made it real. More sad, somehow. Her heart ached for her sister.

Prudence drew in a deep breath and wiped her eyes again. "We all have our crosses to bear, do we not? Sophia has been made to suffer through three seasons before finding the right man, Catherine has had to deal with the loss of a beloved husband, and we all know the horrific struggles you have had to bear, Abby. In truth, I have nothing to complain about. I married a man I love, I get to live in this beautiful home with family nearby and the most wonderful in-laws imaginable. I have one story published, with another in the works, and the most supportive sister and friends in the world. How selfish of me to want more."

Abby pulled her daughter onto her lap and kissed the top of her head. "It's not selfish to want a child, Pru. In fact, it's the most unselfish thing you *could* want. Have you seen a doctor?"

Prudence hugged a pillow to her chest and nodded. "A number of them—both here and in London. They all said the same thing. Everything appears to be in order. Sometimes these things just take time, and sometimes . . ." Her voice drifted off, but she didn't need to finish the sentence. Sophia knew what her sister was thinking.

*Sometimes it isn't in the cards.*

Life could be so backwards at times. A great many children were born to mothers who didn't want them while her sister and Knave, two people who would be the best of parents, were not as blessed.

Sophia wanted to tell her sister not to worry, that it *was* only a matter of time. But what if it wasn't? What if Prudence couldn't bear children of her own? What if Knave would never have a son to carry on his name?

Offering that sort of hope would feel like a lie.

Abby seemed at a loss for words as well, judging by the silence in the room.

Sophia finally gripped her sister's hand tightly and said the only thing she could. "I don't know what trials any of us will have to suffer or how everything is going to work out. I just know it will. Eventually. When all is said and done, I believe God really does know best. You are a good, deserving person, Pru, and I'm certain that one day you will look back on this moment as a setback in a journey worth taking. In the meantime, we are here for you, as you have always been for us."

Prudence blinked at the tears in her eyes and threw her arms around her sister. "Thank you, Soph. You have no idea how much I needed to hear that."

"It's true," Abby agreed. "I wouldn't have Anne or be married to Brigston now if not for a few . . . setbacks. There was a time when I wished I could alter the past and erase certain moments. But I don't think that way anymore. It's as Sophia said. Things will come about as they should in the end. Sometimes all you can do is put your faith in that and move forward."

"I love you both to pieces," said Prudence, wiping more tears from her eyes. Only this time, they seemed to be happy tears. She leaned forward to kiss Anne's cheek and touch Abby's stomach.

"Hello, little one. Are you a boy or a girl?" Prudence closed her eyes and pursed her lips thoughtfully. When she opened them again, she said with all the conviction of a fortune teller, "How perfectly wonderful. It's a boy."

Abby laughed. "Brigston will be overjoyed to hear that."

"As will your mother-in-law," said Sophia. "She certainly dotes on Anne and will do the same with this one."

"I'm sure she will," agreed Abby. "I believe she spends more time in the nursery than she does with us. She's probably there now, wondering who's absconded with little Anne. Which reminds me. It's nearing her nap time. Would you mind terribly if I take her away?"

Prudence made a shooing gesture with her hand. "We all know how quickly her temperament can change when she is hungry or tired. By all means, let the poor girl sleep."

Abby scooted off the bed, brushed a few wrinkles from her afternoon dress, and collected her daughter. "Is it too much to hope that Lord Dagabond won't make an appearance at dinner?"

"Not at all," said Prudence. "I have every faith in Mr. Quinton and our husbands. As of this evening, Lord Dagabond will be no more."

"Hooray," she said.

As soon as she'd slipped out the door, Sophia glanced around the room. "Considering this is Abby's bedchamber, perhaps we should leave as well. I can only imagine what Brigston would think if he walked in to find us here instead of his wife."

Prudence ignored her sister and pulled Scamp close. "I overheard Mother asking about you earlier. She's probably still on the hunt, and she's not likely to look for you in here."

Sophia could imagine the conversation that would eventually take place. *Where have you been all afternoon? What were you thinking, child? That man is not worthy of your notice! Have you forgotten the promise you made to me already?*

*No Mother,* thought Sophia with an inward sigh. *How could I?*

Sophia grabbed a pillow and curled into a ball. "I suppose we could stay a while longer. Should Brigston intrude, we shall just tell him to go away and not breathe a word of our whereabouts to anyone."

Prudence propped her head up with her hand and combed through Scamp's fur. "Speaking of Mother and mysterious whereabouts, where *have* you been all afternoon?"

"Nowhere in particular," said Sophia.

"Oh, come now. You can consider this practice for

when you have to face Mother, which you will. She'll insist on knowing every last detail."

"I shall tell her it is none of her business, as I'm telling you now."

Prudence giggled, her eyes dancing merrily. "You were with Hugh, weren't you? Did he kiss you?"

"What a suggestion, Pru!" Sophia said in scandalized tones. "Of course he did not." *Much to my disappointment,* she added in her mind.

"Ah, I knew you were with him!" Prudence grinned triumphantly. "Did he at least hold your hand? Offer you his coat? Sing in his very off-key voice while waltzing you around a clearing?"

Sophia smiled and shook her head, then rolled onto her back. It was no use hiding it from her sister, nor did she really want to. So many conflicting emotions threatened to boil over inside of her. She could really use a listening ear.

"What am I going to do, Pru? I made a promise to Mother that I'd accept Mr. Fawcett."

"You did *what*?"

Sophia draped an arm over her eyes and sighed. "She promised to stop pushing Lord Dodious on me if I agreed to choose Mr. Fawcett. It seemed a fair compromise at the time."

"Have you learned nothing from me?" Prudence exclaimed. "When it comes to love, you never compromise. Great Jehoshaphat, Soph, what were you thinking?"

Another sigh. "That Hugh and I are an impossibility. Isn't it, Pru? Could I even consider it?"

"Yes and no. I mean no and yes." Prudence crawled to a kneeling position and glared at her sister. "Are you that much of a dunderhead? Of course you should consider him! He's the one, Soph. From that first night in the drawing room, it was obvious to me. You beamed when you recognized him, and you've been beaming ever since. How can you be so blind?"

Sophia *did* feel blind at that moment—probably because her arm still covered her eyes. She removed it and looked at her sister. "That's the point, Pru. I'm trying *not* to be blind. Don't you see? My own sister wouldn't be able to invite us to her family's annual London ball."

Prudence looked at Sophia as though she still thought her a dunderhead. "Whether the ton likes it or not, your name will always be first and foremost on any guest list of mine, as will Hugh's—regardless of whether or not the two of you marry. When have I ever cared a fig for what society thinks?"

It was Sophia's turn to get teary-eyed. Her sister's words meant a great deal. "What would I do without you?"

"Spend the rest of your life as my spinster sister, obviously. You are greatly in my debt, you know. Do you have any idea how long it took Knave to track down Mr. Quinton? Nearly your entire third season. What a blessing he resided in London."

"I knew it." Sophia pointed an accusing finger at her sister. "This was all your doing, wasn't it? You brought Hugh here for me, not Talford."

Her sister nodded. "Knave knew there was probably nothing he could do about Talford, but we had to think of some way to get him here. And it worked, didn't it?" She grinned. "Oh, how I love being right."

Sophia laughed. She would likely never hear the end of this, but at the moment, she was too happy to care. She threw her arms around her sister. "Thank you, Pru. Thank you."

Prudence pulled back and pressed her lips together in thought. "Now we just need to think of a way to extricate you from your promise to Mother."

# FIFTEEN

HUGH STOOD NEAR the fireplace in Lord Knave's study with his elbow propped on the mantle. Although the drapes had been opened, the room still felt dark. A thick layer of clouds had rolled in, making the mahogany desk, bookcases, and burgundy furnishings appear almost black.

Compared to his study back in London, Hugh's current surroundings were lavish—yet another reminder of the differences in their stations.

Lord Knave and Lord Brigston sat on the sofa, frowning at the footman seated across from them. Park stood next to Hugh.

Harry, the footman, tapped his shoes against the rug in a nervous, staccato-like rhythm. His dusty-brown hair looked wild, as though he'd combed his fingers through it one too many times, and his face had a guilty pallor.

Hugh actually felt sorry for the man. One bad decision, and he would lose his livelihood. He'd begged Lord Knave to keep him on, but there were consequences for acting dishonestly, and this was one of them. They'd struck a bargain instead—the footman's testimony in exchange for a reference. Hopefully, the young man had learned his lesson and would never sacrifice his integrity for any amount of money again.

Perhaps Hugh could find a way to help him. Harry *did* seem genuinely sorry.

The door opened, and the butler stepped in to announce Lord Daglum. He walked in arrogantly, looking down his nose at everyone. When his gaze fell upon Park and Harry, his expression turned wary.

*Good,* Hugh thought. *You know you're guilty.*

"Lord Daglum," said Lord Knave. "Good of you to join us. Please, have a seat." He gestured to the one remaining chair in the room, adjacent to the footman. "I believe you already know Harry. And this is Park, an employee of Mr. Quinton's."

Lord Daglum sat down and made a pretense of examining his fingernails. "Is there a reason I am being introduced to two servants?"

The disparaging way he said it made Park stiffen at Hugh's side. Hugh barely refrained from smiling. Angering Park was not an intelligent move.

"As I mentioned before, I believe you already know Harry."

"I can't imagine why I would," said Lord Daglum.

"Perhaps I can refresh your memory," said Hugh, stepping forward. If Lord Daglum decided to call someone out over this business, he didn't want it to be Lord Knave. This had been Hugh's idea, after all.

"You enlisted Harry's help in the game of cards the other evening. He would signal what cards your opponents held, and in return, you would give him ten percent of your profits."

Lord Daglum rolled his eyes. "This is absurd. You couldn't possibly believe the word of a servant over a marquess."

*When that marquess is you, then yes, I can,* Hugh thought. Out loud, he said, "There are other witnesses."

"Who?" Lord Daglum asked. "A maid, perhaps? This gangly fellow here?" He gestured to Park as he rolled his eyes and stood. "If we are finished here, I have other things to attend to."

Hugh had to admit, Lord Daglum was playing his cards well. He knew how to use his title to advantage. It would likely take a miracle to get him to confess his guilt.

Hugh considered his options. He could bluff about having proof. He could threaten to call the magistrate. Or he could throw a solid punch. Judging by Lord Daglum's wiry frame, the man didn't spend much time at Gentleman Jackson's.

That would surely give Lord Daglum reason enough to challenge Hugh to a duel, however, and after this morning's hunting excursion, it was clear who would win at pistols.

"Sit down, Daglum," said Lord Knave, apparently losing patience with the man.

"We have four witnesses willing to stand before a magistrate. We have the money you paid Harry for his part in the scheme. And we have your own sorry excuse for a character. Any man capable of brutally injuring an innocent dog, marquess or not, will not incur much sympathy. As you well know, we have several witnesses to that unhappy affair."

For the first time since entering the room, Lord Daglum swallowed nervously.

*Bravo, Lord Knave,* Hugh inwardly applauded. Even if he'd thought to say the same, coming from him, the words wouldn't have carried the same weight.

"I have a note as well," Harry squeaked. "From his valet. Threatening me into silence." From the way his voice trembled, Hugh knew it had taken a great deal of courage for him to speak out.

*Well done Harry,* he thought. *You're on your way.*

Aside from giving the footman a murderous glare, Lord Daglum said nothing.

Lord Brigston cleared his throat and glanced at Hugh. "What do you suggest we do with him, Mr. Quinton? Turn the matter over to a magistrate? Escort him off the premises immediately? See to it that all of London learns of his duplicity? You are the most compassionate soul present. What is the Christian thing to do?"

"Feed him to the dogs," said Hugh.

Park, Lord Knave, and Lord Brigston chuckled while Harry stared at him, aghast.

"I was only jesting, Harry," said Hugh. "I would never treat an animal as cruelly as that." He would let the others decide to which animal he was referring—Lord Daglum or the dogs.

Hugh folded his arms and amended his earlier sentence. "I suppose if he does the honorable thing and returns the money he stole, along with an apology, we need not involve the magistrate. Perhaps he can be allowed to stay one additional night as well, since these things take time. I'm certain he'll wish to take dinner in his room, however. Then at first light, I will be happy to see that he makes a speedy departure. As to alerting all of London of his duplicity, I will leave that up to the both of you."

Lord Knave raised a questioning eyebrow at Lord Brigston, who nodded in return.

"As much as I would have liked to feed him to the dogs," said Lord Knave, "your suggestion sounds reasonable enough. What do you have to say, Daglum?"

The man's jaw clenched, and he stared daggers at Lord Knave. "I would rather die than spend another night in this—this hovel. I will pack my things and leave immediately."

"Only after you've written at least one note of apology to Mr. Gifford," Lord Brigston reminded him. "And if we are not all repaid every penny of what you took, it's the magistrate who will be hunting you down."

Lord Daglum stood and angrily stormed from the room.

After a moment or two, it was Park who spoke. "Want me to take care of 'im? I'm no Christian."

Lord Brigston barked out a laugh, and Lord Knave chuckled. Hugh shook his head. "I'd rather not see you brought before a magistrate, Park. Let this one go. Men like him dig their own graves eventually."

Lord Knave reached for the decanter and began to pour. "Anyone care for a drink?"

Harry slowly pushed himself up. "I need to pack as well, my lord. If you'll excuse me." He walked the walk of a broken man. Hugh had seen it many times before, and it always wrenched his heart. He wanted to say, *If you let this make you a better man, you'll come about all right,* but it wasn't his place.

Lord Knave must have had a similar thought. When Harry reached the door, he said, "That was brave of you to speak out, Harry. If you maintain your integrity, you'll have no regrets in life. Remember that."

"I will. I am truly sorry, my lord."

"I believe you." He paused. "I have, er . . . heard the Winthrop place is on the hunt for a footman. Perhaps you could inquire there."

Harry seemed to straighten a little. "I'm undeserving of your kindness, my lord, but . . . thank you."

As soon as Harry quit the room, Hugh lifted his glass to Lord Knave. "I believe Lord Brigston was wrong when he gave me credit for being the most compassionate."

"Don't let him fool you," said Lord Brigston. "Earlier

this week, he trounced on me in archery and wasn't the least bit sorry."

"Nor will I ever be." Lord Knave chuckled before downing his brandy.

# SIXTEEN

SOPHIA HELD HER breath as she entered the drawing room. A glance around revealed no Lord Daglum, but perhaps something had detained him. *Please say he is gone,* she thought.

Catherine stood near Knave, Prudence, Abby, and Brigston while the dowager Lady Brigston conversed quietly with Sophia's parents and Lord and Lady Bradden. Only Hugh, and perhaps Lord Daglum, were still at large.

"He's gone," Prudence's voice whispered in Sophia's ear, making her jump.

"Heavens, Pru, must you startle me like that?"

"If you had been paying attention, you would have seen me approach."

Sophia had to admit the purple gown her sister wore definitely drew attention. It was a wonder she hadn't noticed.

Then another thought struck, and she grabbed her sister's arm. "Who's gone?"

"Who do you think?" Prudence grinned. "Lord Daga-bond, obviously."

Sophia let out a relieved breath. For a moment she'd worried it had been Hugh. But no, it was the odious Lord D who would not be joining them this evening. Thank heavens.

"Truly?"

"I would never jest about such matters."

Sophia couldn't help the grin that came to her face. Bless Hugh for coming to Oxfordshire, for becoming the man she'd always suspected he would, and for calling out a cheat and sending him packing.

"I feel so . . . so free," Sophia said, wanting to hug her sister.

Movement caught the corner of her eye, and she looked over to see Hugh walk into the room. He looked resplendent in buff breeches, with a navy coat and matching cravat. As he approached, she caught a whiff of sandalwood, and her grin widened at the familiarity of it—at the familiarity of *him*.

Heedless of her parents or anyone else, she reached out and took both of his hands in her own.

"How can I ever thank you?" she said quietly, feeling overcome by gratitude and tenderness. She looked over his handsome features, noting the creases at the edges of his eyes, the warmth of his touch, and the goodness of his character. How had she managed to come by such a friend?

*I love you,* she thought, feeling the truth of it warm her bones. How strange she felt, like flying and falling and twirling all at once, like she could take on the entire world and come away the victor.

Did he feel it too?

*Say you do,* her expression pleaded. *Say you love me too.*

"'Twas nothing, Miss Gifford." He carefully extracted his hands from hers and glanced around the room, appearing uncomfortable.

He didn't smile or look at her with longing. He didn't even ask if he could take her in to dinner. What he *did* do was give her arm a brotherly pat, step around her, and move to where Knave and Brigston stood with Abby and Catherine.

Sophia remained rooted to the spot, wondering if this was how a candle felt after being snuffed out. The light in the room seemed to dim, and coldness wrapped around her, making her shiver.

She made the mistake of catching the stony stare of her mother and swallowed. Oh dear. After disappearing all afternoon, along with her recent besiege of Hugh, she was undoubtedly in for a lecture, and a lengthy one at that. She could already hear the words, *I held up my end of the bargain. Now it is your turn.*

That horrid promise. Why had Sophia ever agreed to such a thing? Hugh had been right to put an end to their little moment. Her emotions had probably been obvious to everyone. She must really learn to keep herself in check.

The clock chimed the hour, signaling that dinner would shortly begin, and Sophia glanced at the door, hoping to see the butler.

"Will Lord Daglum be joining us?" Her father's voice sounded loud in the quiet.

Knave shook his head. "Some urgent business required his attention in London. He left about an hour ago." The news actually seemed to disappoint her father, and perhaps her mother as well.

"Pity," said her father. "I wanted to thank him for the note he sent around earlier. He actually returned the blunt he won at cards the other evening. Can you believe it? Said he didn't feel right keeping it. Jolly good of him if you ask me."

Sophia rolled her eyes. How like Lord Dodious to make himself appear altruistic when he was anything but. It was a good thing he'd fled to London or she might have given him a good tongue-lashing. Now *that* was a scene she wouldn't mind making.

"Perhaps we misjudged him," said her mother, looking pointedly at Sophia.

*Oh no, we did not,* Sophia thought. Out loud, she said, "I can't help but wonder, Mother, why he didn't feel good about keeping his winnings. That seems a little odd, don't you think? Unless he had reason not to, of course."

Her mother didn't have the chance to respond. The butler cleared his throat, probably to announce dinner, but when Sophia turned around, she forgot all about food, Hugh, and the odious Lord Dagabond.

"I'm pleased to announce that Mr. Fawcett has returned," said the butler. "Lord Bradden, dinner is ready whenever you are."

Lord Bradden nodded at the butler before extending a hand to Mr. Fawcett. "This is an unexpected pleasure. It is good to see you again, sir."

Mr. Fawcett didn't have the look of a man who'd traveled from Surrey. He wore dark breeches, a white shirt, and a light blue coat, with a pristinely tied cravat. One would think he'd ridden over from a neighboring estate.

While everyone else cheerfully greeted him. Sophia couldn't move or speak. How many emotions would she be made to experience in one day? She was glad to see him, she was, but . . . How would she possibly tell him her feelings had changed, that he'd returned to Radbourne for no reason? How would she tell her mother that she could no longer keep her promise?

Then there was Hugh—the man she loved, who'd only just dismissed her. What if he had no intention of coming up to scratch? What if he would be the next guest to leave? What if—

"I was hoping to arrive before dinner was called," he said, casting a grin in Sophia's direction. "I stopped at the nearest inn to clean myself up a bit and sent word ahead, but your butler has informed me that my note must have gone astray. I apologize for appearing unannounced."

Knave clapped him on the shoulder. "Good to have you back, Mr. Fawcett. Charades has not been nearly as amusing since you left."

Mr. Fawcett chuckled as he approached Sophia, looking almost shy. "What about you, Miss Gifford? Are you happy to see me?"

She could only nod. Her shoes felt glued to the spot, so long had she stood there. Her mind and tongue felt stuck as well, though she managed to finally ask, "How is your sister, sir?"

He shook his head the way a father of a troublesome child might do. "Well enough, I suppose. She suffered what she considered to be a broken heart when our cousin—a man she'd developed a *tendre* for last Christmas—announced his betrothal to another woman. It's a silly matter, really, considering she is not yet sixteen, but she has always had a flair for the dramatic.

"After chiding her for leading me to believe she was ill, I spent several harrowing days convincing her that she would not expire from a wounded heart. I had no idea a girl could shed so many tears."

Sophia wasn't sure how to respond, especially when his tale seemed like a foretelling of what was to come. She may very well wound Mr. Fawcett's heart, and Hugh could easily do the same to hers. Heartbreak, pain, and tears seemed to lie in wait, threatening to erupt if things didn't come about as Sophia desperately wanted them to. She could only pray that, if it came down to it, she'd suffer through the emotions a little less dramatically than his sister.

"Oh, my dear sir," said Mrs. Gifford. "It is a testament to your fortitude and kindness that you cared for her as you did. I hope she is better now. We have all missed your company, Sophia especially."

He smiled and bowed over Sophia's hand. "I have missed you as well, Miss Gifford."

*I am a fraud,* Sophia thought. She felt nothing at his touch. No real warmth to speak of, no tingles, no euphoria, nothing. Well, that wasn't precisely true. She felt an unaccountable anxiety—the same feeling that had plagued her every time he drew near since this house party had begun.

"Would you do the honor of accompanying me into dinner?" he asked.

After a glance in Hugh's direction, she forced herself to say, "Yes."

As Sophia walked alongside him, she was reminded of when she'd first learned to ride. She'd sat nervously atop a pony, subject to the whims of a groom who'd pulled the animal this way and that. It bothered her that she had no control over which way the pony turned or how fast he walked. Not until she'd been given control of the reins did she grow to love riding. The first time she tugged on the leather cord and felt the pony respond, an exhilarating thrill of freedom shot through her. She felt that same fantasy every time she rode—a sort of fantasy that she had some control over her life.

She didn't though, not really. She was essentially back on that pony, at the mercy of Hugh, her mother, Mr. Fawcett and whoever else held the reins. She couldn't force Hugh to make her an offer anymore than she could take back the promise she'd made to her mother or redirect Mr. Fawcett's interest elsewhere.

For Sophia, real independence could only be felt on the back of her horse. Even then, it would only ever be fleeting.

# SEVENTEEN

WHEN SOPHIA ASCENDED the staircase to her bedchamber that evening, she overheard her mother say to her father, "Send for the carriage. I'll be back in a moment."

Sophia briefly thought about fleeing. She could hide in an empty bedchamber, or even closet, until she was certain her mother had gone.

But that would only prolong the inevitable and give her mother even more ammunition to fire at her. No, it was best to get it over with now.

She walked down the hall and into her bedchamber, where she perched on the edge of her bed and calmly waited. As soon as her mother appeared, Sophia started the conversation.

"Before you start in on me, Mother, I already know everything you plan to say. I should not have taken as long of a walk this afternoon, I should not have made that scene in the drawing room before dinner, and I should have paid more attention to Mr. Fawcett. Yes, I caught that look you sent my way. But I am exhausted and want nothing more than to crawl under my bedclothes and sleep until my head no longer feels like it is stuffed with cotton. Can you please forgive my actions today if I promise to do better tomorrow?"

Sophia didn't expect her speech to do much good—her mother wasn't one to get the wind knocked out of her sails so easily—but much to her surprise, no lecture came. Instead, her mother gave a quick nod, as though they had reached an accord. "I told your father I would be back in a moment, and so I shall be. Goodnight, Sophia."

Sophia blinked, not daring to believe it could be that easy. But then her mother paused just outside the door, and Sophia tensed.

"You went on a long walk, you say?"

"Yes."

"On your own?"

Sophia hesitated, not wanting to drag Hugh's name into the conversation. "Scamp was asleep by the fire. I didn't want to wake him." It wasn't a lie. Scamp *had* been asleep by the fire, and she would never wake a sleeping dog. But it hadn't been the full truth either. What did that make it? What did that make her?

Her mother nodded. "He does like his afternoon naps, doesn't he?"

"Almost as much as I like my evening naps." Sophia softened her words with what she hoped was a smile. It was all she could manage.

"You don't have to tell me twice, dear. I shall see you at the picnic tomorrow."

With those parting words, her mother turned around and walked away. Sophia stared at the empty hallway for several moments before slowly closing her door and ringing for her maid. What a strange encounter that had been.

Perhaps she should go on the offensive more often.

WHEN IT CAME to men, there were two moments in Sophia's life she wished she could alter. The first happened several years prior, when she'd brazenly kissed the man she now called her brother-in-law. One would think she would have learned from that first rejection not to throw herself at a man, but that other night in the garden, when Hugh looked so handsome and smelled so wonderful, she'd lost all sense and done it again when she'd essentially asked him to kiss her.

What a slowtop she could be at times. Or, as she preferred to think of it—naively optimistic. It was a good feeling, really—to believe a man might actually *want* to kiss her. But no, she'd gambled on that belief twice now and lost. With Knave, it had been a humiliation. With Hugh, she'd felt pain. Not the sort of pain one felt after stubbing a toe or pricking a finger with a needle. It ran deeper somehow, like a plague on her mind that never let up.

To make matters worse, since Mr. Fawcett's return Hugh had become something of a ghost. Each morning, he'd ride off in the direction of town, where he'd stay for hours. Upon his return, he'd shut himself away in Knave's study until late into the night, sending his regrets for dinner and the evening's entertainments. He didn't picnic with the party or play charades or try his hand at archery. He simply deserted them.

Sophia had no idea what kept him so occupied, but she had a feeling it had more to do with avoiding her than anything else. Why else would he make himself scarce? She must have offended him in some way. Made too much of a spectacle of herself. Did he intend to hide away for the remainder of the house party? If so, why stay at Radbourne at all, other than to torment her?

*A pox be upon all men,* she thought sourly. They'd

brought her nothing but confusion, frustration, embarrassment, and heartache.

Such was her mood these days.

Even out here on Radbourne's veranda, surrounded by beautiful weather and her dearest friends, she couldn't cheer herself up. She spied a horse and rider in the distance and held her breath. But no, it was merely a passerby. Not Hugh.

*Botheration.*

"Wouldn't you agree, Miss Gifford?" Mr. Fawcett's voice cut through her thoughts. Ever since Hugh's desertion, the responsibility of entertaining and escorting both Catherine and Sophia had fallen to the poor man. The fact that Sophia was in a constant state of distraction didn't help matters either.

Thank goodness Catherine was better company. She actually listened to him, replied, and even genuinely laughed at his asides. Sophia was sure he would have found a reason to leave Radbourne if not for her sweet friend.

Mr. Fawcett watched Sophia expectantly, as though waiting for an answer. What had he said again? Oh yes, he asked if she agreed with something—what, she had no idea—but that didn't stop her from nodding and saying, "Yes, of course."

"Really?" He sounded surprised. "I would have thought you, of all people, would disagree."

*For pity's sake,* she thought. *Why ask if you already know my answer?*

Oh well. She couldn't exactly change her mind now. In for a penny, in for pound.

"I can't imagine why you'd think that," she said. "I'm a very agreeable person."

He and Catherine laughed, but it was Catherine who finally explained. "Mr. Fawcett was just saying how the view would be even lovelier without that large tree blocking it. He asked if you agreed that it should be cut down."

Sophia looked at the massive ash tree, with its elegant, sweeping branches and vibrant green leaves. Cut it down? How could he suggest such a thing?

"Have you lost your senses, Mr. Fawcett?" she blurted. "Taking an ax to such a magnificent tree would be criminal."

He grinned and nodded his head at her. "I knew you weren't attending."

She sighed, realizing too late that he had only been teasing her. He wouldn't want that tree cut down anymore than the next person. "No, I gather not. For that I'm truly sorry."

He took a sip of tea and carefully set down the cup. "You've seemed a little preoccupied since my return. Is something troubling you?"

A *little* was putting it kindly—which was exactly the sort of person Mr. Fawcett was. Kind. Circumspect. A gentleman through and through.

She shook her head, giving him an honest answer this time. "I've merely been stewing over things I have no control over."

"Talford Hall?" he guessed.

Since it was partly true, she nodded.

He covered her hand with his and gave it a squeeze. "It's going to be all right, Miss Gifford. You'll see."

Sophia had to laugh at his words, which actually felt good. "I told my sister much the same thing the other day. I suppose that makes me a hypocrite for not taking my own advice."

"It makes you human," he said.

Why, oh why, couldn't she feel more for this man than friendship? It made no sense. He was truly the best of men, and she was truly the stupidest of women.

"You are too kind, Mr. Fawcett," she said, feeling lighter

all of a sudden. The conversation and resulting laughter had freed her from her melancholy. She was ready to have some fun.

She stood and looked at the beauty surrounding them. The grass practically begged to be stepped upon. "Pru, do you have rackets and a shuttlecock lying around? I feel the urge to play a game."

"What a brilliant idea," said Prudence. "Yes, let's do it."

# EIGHTEEN

THE MORNING OF the soirée dawned gray and drizzly. Sophia frowned at the clouds from her bedroom window and wondered if it would remain this gloomy all day.

Movement caught her eye, and Sophia looked to see Hugh galloping through the rain towards the road. He had a satchel slung over one shoulder and, judging by his breakneck pace, was late to something or trying to outrun the rain. Sophia reminded herself, yet again, that he wasn't accountable to her—and never would be—but that didn't keep her from wondering where he went each day and for what reason. He'd only told Knave that some urgent business matters had arisen that he needed to address.

She let the curtains drop and hugged her arms to her chest. It was early yet, but there was no sense in crawling back into bed and stewing over things she couldn't change. Best to get on with her day and try to forget about Hugh and his mysterious errands.

An hour later, Catherine arrived early as planned to help Abby with the floral arrangements. Sophia made herself useful as well, needing the distraction like a bird needed to fly, but she had never been good at grouping flowers in a pleasing manner. Instead, she busied herself cutting and preparing the stems for those who knew what to do with them.

Trouble was, no matter what she did or who she spoke with, thoughts of Hugh pestered her mind and tried her patience.

"Sophia, isn't this gorgeous?" Abby pointed at a large bouquet that Catherine was arranging in a silver vase. "I had no idea you were so talented, Catherine."

"It *is* stunning," Sophia agreed. "As is yours, Abby. You have both made me very glad I took on the invitations rather than the flowers. Once word gets out about your talents, which it certainly will tonight, everyone in the county will ask you to make their bouquets."

"'Tis a good thing I will be leaving shortly," said Abby with a grin.

"Don't remind me," said Sophia. "Can you not stay for another few weeks at least?"

Abby shook her head. "We've been away long enough. Brigston is growing anxious to check on things at the estate, and I . . ." She ran a hand across her belly and smiled. "I have some sewing to do."

"I shall come for a visit as soon as the babe arrives," Sophia promised.

"You had better all come," said Abby. "I will be aching for my friends by that point."

"Count me in," said Catherine as she prodded another fern leaf into her arrangement.

Sophia watched her work, almost mesmerized that someone could take a handful of random leaves and flowers and make them look so beautiful.

"Poor Catherine," Sophia said. "Unlike Abby, you have no escape. You should prepare yourself for an onslaught. I have heard that Mrs. Hilliard is planning a country dance at her home in a few weeks. After seeing that creation tonight, she will certainly solicit your talents."

"I would actually like that," said Catherine. "I could use a new pastime in my life."

"As could I," said Mr. Fawcett, striding into the room with a grin. He had seemed more chipper of late—or perhaps he just seemed that way because Sophia had been more glum. Either way, he looked well.

"To what pastime are you referring, Mrs. Harper?" he asked.

She gestured to the bouquet she'd created and dimpled up at him. "What do you say, sir? Care to give it a go?"

He bit his lower lip and eyed it skeptically. "Perhaps a different pastime would suit me better."

"Such as?" Abby asked.

"If I recall"—Catherine inserted another stem into her arrangement—"you are quite good at charades. Perhaps you could take up pantomiming."

"Yes, I could be good at that." He made a few hand gestures, as though struggling to climb a rope, and all the ladies laughed at his comical expressions.

Not for the first time, Sophia wondered where this side of Mr. Fawcett had been hiding. Back in London, he had been much more reserved. Perhaps the country air brought it out of him.

"On second thought," said Catherine, "I think pantomiming should be saved for those who don't have a pleasing voice or a charming laugh. You should look into acting instead."

He straightened and tugged on his coat in a prideful way. "Why, thank you, Mrs. Harper. I believe I will talk a great deal more now."

"And laugh," Sophia added.

"That too." He nodded.

"I will rescind the compliment, sir, if it puffs you up," Catherine teasingly scolded.

"Even if it is only a little?" he asked.

"Perhaps a *very* little would be all right."

"Then I shall accept your compliment with gratitude and try my best not to become too boastful when I speak or laugh." He smiled warmly at Catherine while Sophia continued to study him in curiosity. Honestly, who was this man? He'd always been kind and congenial, but before this house party, she would have never described him as humorous or engaging. Something had changed.

When he glanced in her direction and caught her watching him, he stiffened, blushed slightly, and cleared his throat, reverting back to his old self. "Perhaps I have talked too much already."

Sophia realized then that she'd probably been gaping at him. Oh dear. She quickly wiped the astonishment from her face. "Please don't, sir. I quite like you this way."

Her words didn't have the desired effect. Instead of bringing back his smile, they seemed to make him more uncomfortable. After a brief, awkward silence, he tucked his hands behind his back in a formal manner.

"Miss Gifford," he said, "I have heard that Lady Bradden has a pretty conservatory somewhere. Do you, by chance, know where it is?"

"I do," she said, perplexed by the sudden shift in him. "Would you like me to show you?"

"Please."

As they walked from the ballroom, the awkward silence continued. Sophia didn't know what to make of it. Conversation had always been an easy thing between them in the past, but now everything felt different.

When they reached the conservatory, she finally confronted him. "Is something the matter, Mr. Fawcett? If I have offended you, I—"

"No, no." He held out his hand to stop her, looking distressed. "You have done nothing of the sort. If anything, I am the one at fault."

Sophia blinked at him, uncomprehending. "At fault for what, precisely? I assure you, sir, you have done nothing to cause me offense."

He sighed and shook his head as though she'd misunderstood. Then he carefully took her hands in his and looked her in the eye. "I'm doing a poor job of this, aren't I?"

*A poor job of what?* she thought in confusion.

"Sophia . . . May I call you Sophia?"

"Of course." She dropped her gaze to their clasped hands and had the sudden realization that he was about to make her an offer of marriage. The romantic room. Her Christian name. The quiet, nervous way he spoke.

*Oh dear.*

Her body began to tremble as the promise she'd made to her mother pounded in her ears. Could she say yes to this man? Could she be happy with him? Could she make *him* happy?

*No.* The truth of it struck her like it never had before. She couldn't do any of it. Even if Hugh walked out of her life, she still couldn't marry Mr. Fawcett.

He pulled her over to a bench in the corner and sat beside her. "Sophia, I—"

"Mr. Fawcett, I know what you're going to say," she blurted, frantically trying to think of a way to stop him. If he never proposed, she wouldn't be guilty of breaking her promise to her mother.

"You do?" He blinked in surprise.

Why did life have to be so complicated at times? Why couldn't everyone fall in love with the right person? Why did there have to be frustration, misunderstandings, and broken hearts? It served no purpose to injure a good man like Mr. Fawcett.

"Have you already spoken with my father?" Sophia asked quietly, hoping against hope his answer would be no.

His brow furrowed in confusion. "He has not come to Radbourne this morning, so . . . no. Is there a reason I *should* speak with him?"

Now it was Sophia's turn to be confused. Perhaps he didn't see the need to ask her father because she was of age. Or perhaps she had this all wrong.

"Mr. Fawcett—"

"Please, call me Jacob."

"Jacob then," she said. Goodness, how to delicately phrase this? "Er . . . Are you . . ." No, she couldn't ask that. The point was to *keep* him from proposing, not encourage it. If, indeed, that's what this was. She was beginning to have her doubts.

"Am I what?" he asked.

Drat it all, she needed to speak plainly. "Sir, if you are attempting to make me an offer of marriage, you mustn't."

"Make you an off—oh, blast. Is that what you think I'm doing?"

"Aren't you?"

"Er . . . no." He released her hands and stood, scratching at the back of his head. "I can't deny that I had every intention of doing just that, but . . . Devil take it. There is no easy way to say this." He paused and looked at her. "Hold up. Did you just say I mustn't propose?"

"Yes."

"Why?"

176

"Because you do not love me."

His eyes widened. "I . . . don't?"

"Well, do you?" Good grief. They were circling around each other like two nitwits. Any more of this and Sophia would go mad.

"No. I mean—I like you. I'm very fond of you, but . . ."

"You do not love me."

He grimaced. "Er . . . no. I once thought I did. You are so kind and beautiful and—"

"Mr. Fawcett—"

"Jacob."

She sighed, then managed a smile. "Jacob, there is no need to list the reasons you should care for me but don't."

"But I *do* care for you."

"Just not enough to offer for me."

He hesitated and furrowed his brow. "Would you . . . like me to offer for you?"

"No!" Heaven help her. "I suppose I should tell you that I feel the same. We have become good friends, but that is all."

His shoulders sagged in relief. "I cannot tell you how glad I am to hear you say that."

"And I cannot tell you how glad I am that we finally understand one another."

He laughed and, when she patted the bench at her side, took a seat.

"Tell me," she said. "What has changed?"

He leaned back and draped an arm across the spine of the bench. "Catherine," he said.

Sophia's mouth fell open, but as she thought over the past several days, everything became clear. His newfound sense of humor, his increased confidence, his chipper personality—the change had nothing to do with the country and everything to do with her friend. Only it wasn't really a change, was it? With Catherine, Jacob could simply be himself.

"Does she feel the same?" Sophia asked.

He shrugged. "I cannot say. The situation has been a little . . . complicated. You understand. It's the reason I orchestrated our little *tête-à-tête* this morning. Gads, I was so worried you'd think me an utter cad."

"Fickle, perhaps. Not a cad." She smiled to show she was only jesting.

"I suppose that's marginally better. You truly don't think ill of me?"

She shook her head. "I can't believe I didn't see it before. It's so apparent now. Catherine is a much better fit for you than I could ever be. But I must say," she teased, "you have set your sights rather high."

It was fun to interact with him in this way—at least *she* thought so. Jacob, on the other hand, appeared suddenly discouraged.

He exhaled and let his head fall backward in a somewhat dramatic gesture. "Don't I know it."

Sophia tried not to take offense that he so obviously placed Catherine on a higher pedestal than herself, but his admission still stung a little. A silly reaction, really, considering Catherine *was* a better catch.

"Perhaps I can be of assistance," Sophia offered.

He slowly lifted his head, followed by his brow. "In what way?"

She gave the matter some thought before answering. "I could let it slip—in a casual way, of course—that you and I have determined we will not suit after all. Catherine's reaction could be quite telling."

He pursed his lips before slowly nodding. "I'll admit, it

would be nice to know how she might take such tidings—even if she is impassive."

"Let us hope she responds with pleasure, shall we?"

He chuckled a little, but the sound didn't contain much humor. "Hope can be a frightening thing, Sophia. The moment a person decides to embrace it is the moment a coin is tossed on his or her happiness."

"But haven't you already tossed that coin?" Sophia asked. "When you made the decision to speak with me and . . . clarify our relationship, you chose to cling to hope, did you not?"

"I suppose it was a step in that direction."

"Then why not embrace it and see where you land?" With any luck, it would carry him to a happier place than she had been plopped when she'd chosen to hope for a positive outcome with Hugh.

He looked at her gratefully. "Why not, indeed. But first, let us see how she reacts to your news. A man needs at least a little assurance before he tosses that coin."

Sophia laughed. How good it felt to focus on something other than her own sorrows, even if that something made her a little envious. Perhaps it would be a good thing she and her parents would need to remove themselves from Talford shortly. Having a blissfully happy sister on one side and an equally happy friend on the other would be a difficult cross to bear.

Then again, now that Sophia had exhausted all possible marriage prospects, she and her parents may very well be at the mercy of her sister.

Probably best not to dwell on that just yet.

At least she was now free from the promise she'd made to her mother. That was something she *could* dwell on—and would.

"Jacob," she said carefully, "I wonder if you would do me a favor."

"Anything," came his reply.

Sophia felt an inkling of guilt at what she was about to request. It wasn't exactly fair to ask this of him, but . . . well, sometimes life wasn't fair.

"Do you think you could somehow inform my father and mother—particularly my mother—that you have decided we will not suit after all?"

He didn't even hesitate. "Of course. I would be a cad not to agree when you have so kindly offered to do the same with Catherine. Your parents have never been partial to my suit anyway. I'm certain to bring them glad tidings."

More guilt followed. Perhaps it was wrong for her not to correct his misconception, but it would be better for him to approach her parents with a positive attitude than one of fear, wouldn't it?

How far she had fallen in so little time.

"Thank you, Jacob."

"My pleasure, Sophia."

# NINETEEN

SOPHIA RETURNED TO the ballroom to find Catherine and Abby putting the finishing touches on the floral arrangements. Prudence had joined them as well, directing where she wanted each bouquet placed.

"I think that one would look best on that pedestal near the balcony doors, don't you, Abby?"

Abby didn't seem to hear her friend. She'd caught sight of Sophia and was giving her a look that said, *Well? Is there something you wish to tell us?*

When Sophia failed to respond to the unasked question, Abby twirled a fern leaf between her fingers and casually said, "That was a lengthy trip to the conservatory, Soph. Did you get lost?"

Was it Sophia's imagination or did Catherine suddenly seem anxious or nervous or . . . something? The frenzied way she fiddled with the stems on a perfectly lovely arrangement made Sophia wonder.

Prudence ceased talking and glanced at each of the women in confusion. She must have determined that something was amiss because she finally folded her arms and stared pointedly at Abby. "What did I miss?"

"I'm not sure," said Abby. "I was hoping Sophia could tell us."

Sophia only shrugged. "Tell you what?"

"For crying out loud," said Abby. "Are you, or are you not betrothed? Catherine seems to think that was the reason Mr. Fawcett spirited you away. Or did he really wish to be shown the conservatory?"

Sophia glanced at Catherine, but her friend continued to busy herself with the arrangement on the table in front of her, her expression blank. She didn't even pause or look up when Abby asked about a possible betrothal.

Prudence, on the other hand, had taken a keen interest. "She couldn't possibly be betrothed to Mr. Fawcett. It's Mr. Quinton she loves."

Sophia rolled her eyes, choosing to ignore her sister. This conversation wasn't meant to be about her.

"Catherine," she said instead, "you are going to damage those poor stems if you keep shuffling them around like that. The arrangement is perfect."

Catherine paused to examine her efforts. "I was thinking I should add another pink lily or two. What do you think?"

Abby reached across the table and picked up the arrangement, balancing it on her hip. "I think I would like to know whether or not Sophia has some news to share."

All three women looked at Sophia, but it was her sister who lost patience first. "Honestly, Soph, this isn't a difficult question to answer. Did Mr. Fawcett ask for your hand?"

Sophia debated about letting them think he had, only to discard the idea. If Catherine had any feelings at all for Jacob, that would be a cruel thing to do.

"No. He did not make me an offer nor will he. We simply discussed our . . . situation and concluded that we will only ever be good friends."

From the corner of her eye, Sophia watched Catherine,

but other than a slight widening of her eyes, she remained impassive. Sophia wanted to groan in frustration. *Catherine, do you or do you not care that Jacob is a free man?* she wanted to demand.

"I don't understand," said Abby. "Why come all this way—twice, I might add—if he didn't feel anything more than friendship towards you?"

"He thought he did, but I believe he has developed tender feelings for . . . another, and"—lest anyone pity her—"I suppose I have as well." Much good it did her.

Prudence waved aside Sophia's explanation with an impatient flip of her wrist. "I'm not sure why we are having this conversation. We all know Sophia is over the moon for Mr. Quinton, and it is obvious Mr. Fawcett has grown fond of Catherine. What we *should* be discussing is how to encourage Mr. Quinton to come up to scratch."

When Sophia saw the look of horror on Catherine's face, she nearly laughed. If anything could produce a reaction, it was her sister's plain speaking. And oh, did it produce a reaction.

"What are you saying, Pru?" Catherine spluttered. "Mr. Fawcett isn't fond of me. He's fond of Sophia!"

Sophia tried extra hard not to smile, but it was a trial. "I believe we already clarified that he isn't, Catherine, which is actually a relief. Though he is everything a woman could hope to find in a man, I am not in love with him."

Catherine grew more agitated by the moment. She couldn't seem to catch her breath, and her fingers fiddled with the gold locket around her neck.

"You're wrong," she said. "Mr. Fawcett couldn't possibly care for me, and I . . . I am still in love with Stephen. I always will be."

*Ah, so that was the issue.* Catherine didn't want to be disloyal to her late husband's memory.

Sophia approached her friend with a sympathetic look. "Stephen's likeness is in that locket you always wear, isn't it?"

"Yes," she breathed.

"Of course you still love him."

"With all my heart."

Sophia chose her next words carefully. "I believe hearts are magical things, capable of expanding to include all those we grow to care for, be it a child, a friend, or another man." Sophia gave Catherine's hand a squeeze. "He would want you to be happy, you know."

"I know, but . . . I hardly know Mr. Fawcett."

"And he hardly knows you," Sophia said. "I don't think he is ready for any sort of commitment just yet, if that's what concerns you. I'm sure all he wants is the opportunity to know you better."

"But he's leaving in a few days."

"That can be easily remedied," inserted Prudence. "I'll simply tell him he is welcome to stay for as long as he likes. But only if you wish it, Catherine."

Sophia felt like rolling her eyes all over again. "Since when have you taken the wishes of others into consideration, Pru?"

"Since now," said Prudence. "Only look at the poor girl. She's as skittish as a newborn kitten. Forgive me, Catherine, I mean no offense."

"None taken." Catherine's hand dropped from her locket to her stomach. "I *am* skittish. Very skittish, in fact. I may become ill."

"It is only nerves," said Abby. "Take several deep breaths and try to calm yourself. No one is forcing you to feel a certain way or do anything. As you said, Mr. Fawcett will be going in a few days. If you do not care for him, nothing must be done. He will take his leave, and you'll never have to see him again."

Catherine did as Abby suggested and inhaled deeply. After a few moments, she seemed to collect herself. "Mr. Fawcett *is* charming, and I *do* like him, but up until now, I was under the impression he came here to woo Sophia, not me. I need time to sort through everything. Perhaps I shouldn't come this evening. With the way I'm feeling, I will probably make things very awkward."

"No," Sophia said. "The sooner you face him, the sooner you can put this awkwardness behind you. Just pretend as though this conversation never occurred."

Abby and Prudence nodded in agreement.

"But it *did* occur," Catherine said.

"Yes, but he doesn't know that, does he?"

Sophia's words didn't seem to help. Catherine began to fret over her lower lip and grow anxious once again.

Sophia gave Catherine's hand another squeeze. "I don't know what the answer is either. What I do know is that Jacob is a different man when you are around. He's happier and more himself. You bring out the best in him. What you need to determine, my sweet friend, is whether or not he does the same for you. So cast your fears aside and come tonight, and when Jacob asks for a dance, which he will, smile and let yourself enjoy the moment for what it is—a dance between two friends who would like to become better acquainted."

Catherine nodded haphazardly, as though she was trying to convince herself that's precisely what she should do.

"Yes. You are right. I should come, and I will. But . . . oh my goodness, what shall I wear?"

Prudence and Abby said, almost in unison, "Your sapphire gown," making everyone laugh, including Catherine. Her eyes sparkled in a way they hadn't in a while, and she seemed . . . happier.

In that brief, lovely moment, Sophia felt like everything was right in the world—or at least, almost.

HUGH FOLLOWED THE butler down the long, dark hallway at Talford. Only one small window at the end offered light to the area, and it wasn't much to speak of. Footsteps echoed throughout, sounding loud and eerie in the silence.

The butler preceded him into the library and announced, "Mr. Quinton has arrived, sir," before stepping aside to allow Hugh entrance.

Hugh had been expecting to see only Mr. Gifford in the room, but Mrs. Gifford was also present, seated on a high-backed chair near the empty fireplace. She directed a cold look at him, as though he was the last person she wished to see. Judging by her husband's grim expression, he felt the same.

Hugh wanted to turn on his heel and quit the room, taking with him the contract he carried. He might have done just that, if not for the reminder that he was here for Sophie—not them. She was the only person who mattered, so he set aside his pride and remained.

Mr. Gifford didn't offer Hugh a drink or even a seat. He got straight to the point. "If you are here to ask for my daughter's hand, Mr. Quinton, you are on a fool's errand. She is not meant for the likes of you."

The likes of him. Hugh gritted his teeth, despising men like Mr. Gifford—those who saw people for their possessions and status, instead of their character. He and his wife would rather their daughter marry a selfish boor like Lord Daglum than a good, honest man who truly cared for her.

In a way, Hugh felt sorry for them. They were caught in a world that expected perfection and would spend their entire lives trying to achieve the impossible.

Thank goodness Sophie knew better.

Hugh tapped the folder he held on his palm. "If I *had* come to ask for Sophie's hand, it would only be a formality. Or have you forgotten that she is of age and does not need your permission to marry?"

"How dare you speak to me in that manner, you insufferable—"

"Mr. Quinton," his wife interrupted in a calmer voice. "Do you mean to say you are not here to declare your intentions for our daughter?"

"No."

"Then why have you come?"

He examined the folder he carried, wishing he could have taken it to Sophie instead of her parents, but it was her father who controlled Talford at this time, not her. Best he deal directly with Mr. Gifford.

He tossed the folder on the table in front of Mr. Gifford before taking the seat across from him.

Mr. Gifford eyed the folder with distain. "What's that?"

"It's an agreement for you to purchase a parcel of land about an hour's ride north of here. It has rich, well drained soil and would make an ideal location for at least fifteen tenant farms. I'm the first to admit, it's unorthodox to acquire land unconnected to one's existing property, but it could be a solution to make Talford self-sustaining again, perhaps the only solution. By investing in this land and new farms, you could turn your estate around."

Mr. Gifford didn't respond. He stared at the paperwork, his brow furrowed.

It was his wife who finally said, "You obviously know of our financial struggles, Mr. Quinton. Did Sophia make you aware of them?"

"No," he answered. "It was Lord Knave who came to me for help."

"Knave requested *your* help?" spluttered an indignant Mr. Gifford. "Why would he do such a thing?"

"Because that's what I do, Mr. Gifford. I teach people like you how to better manage their estates. At the risk of sounding boastful, I'm quite good at it too. Lord Knave knew this and sought out my services. It's the reason he invited me to the house party. He wished for me to look into Talford's dealings and see if anything could be done to alter the situation."

This revelation only served to agitate Mr. Gifford further. He stood and began pacing the room, his hands balled into fists. "My own son-in-law went behind my back? How dare he do such a thing! Why was I not told of this before now?"

Hugh gripped the arms of his chair, trying his best to maintain his composure. He'd known his share of pompous, ungrateful men, but after poring over numbers, making several visits to the property in question, and reading through numerous revisions of this contract until his eyes were too bleary to continue, one would think Mr. Gifford would show at least a little gratitude, at the very least some restraint.

"I believe," said Hugh stiffly, "Lord Knave knew something of the history between you and my father and realized I'd be the last person you'd approach for help."

"He was correct." Mr. Gifford continued to stomp about the room, making his displeasure known.

Mrs. Gifford, on the other hand, seemed to warm a bit. "Mr. Quinton, I don't understand how this could save Talford. If you're aware of our struggles, you must also know we haven't the funds to invest in additional land."

"*You* may not, but if Sophia marries Mr. Fawcett by the year's end—he would have to agree to the terms, of course—

her dowry could cover the costs. Several things will need to happen for everything to play out as needed, but it *can* work."

Silence ensued. Even Mr. Gifford stopped his angry pacing while Mrs. Gifford studied Hugh, her expression cloudy with uncertainty. "I don't understand. Why go to all of this trouble for us? Do you expect a payment of some sort? A share of the profits?"

Hugh couldn't blame her suspicions. Anyone in her situation might wonder the same.

"Under normal circumstances, I do ask for a small share, with the understanding that I would continue to act as an advisor when needed, but in this situation, I ask for nothing.

"I didn't come here to help either of you. I came to help Sophie. Years ago, she was a friend to me when I had none, and this is my way of returning her many kindnesses. It was actually her suggestion to create new tenant farms. I just discovered a way to make it work."

Hugh could practically see the battle waging in Mr. Gifford's mind. Hugh—a man he despised—stood before him, freely offering aid. He probably wanted to take the papers and toss them into the fire, then toss Hugh out on his ear. Instead, he said nothing.

Mrs. Gifford sat back and laid her hands across her lap. The room had grown so quiet, the purple taffeta gown she wore made a rustling sound.

"I don't know what to say," she said at last. "I had been so certain you were making arrangements for a special license and intended to steal our Sophia away. But . . . well, I was wrong. Forgive me, Mr. Quinton. It seems we are in your debt."

"Agreed," Hugh said with a small smile, earning a glare

from Mr. Gifford and a raised eyebrow from Mrs. Gifford. "Which is why I have taken the liberty of adding one contingency to the contract."

He rifled through the papers until he found the correct one, then pointed to the last paragraph. "For the sale of this land to go through, you must agree to involve Sophie in all future business dealings regarding the estate. Any decisions, be it how much money is allocated for supplies or whether or not farmland should be sold will require both of your signatures. She has a keen mind and could be a valuable asset if you will allow her to assist you. Talford will one day fall to her, after all. It is only right she should have a say in the managing of it."

Mr. Gifford said nothing, but the cold, hard look in his eyes conveyed his loathing at being controlled in this manner, especially by someone who was not his equal. Hugh couldn't blame him, really. Pride was a difficult beast to manage, no matter one's station. Like it or not, though, Mr. Gifford would do well to take Hugh's advice.

Having said all he'd come to say, Hugh stood. "Please look over those documents and contact me if any questions arise. Keep in mind that I will be leaving for London first thing tomorrow morning."

Mrs. Gifford stood as well. "Am I correct in assuming you will be at the soirée tonight, Mr. Quinton?"

"Yes."

She nodded, looking neither pleased nor displeased by the news. Hugh had to admire her poise. "Then we shall see you this evening. Good day to you, and thank you again."

With those parting words, Hugh strode down the long, dark hallway and out into a damp and drizzly afternoon. He put on his hat and tugged on his gloves before descending the steps.

Only one thing left to do.

# TWENTY

IN HER BEDCHAMBER with the door closed, Sophia could hear the musicians warming up in the ballroom. They sounded remarkably loud from where she sat at her dressing table, and every now and then she could feel the floor vibrate beneath her feet.

*How wonderful,* she thought dryly. *My room happens to be located directly over the ballroom.* Now, if she were to plead a headache and retire early, as she may very well do, she wouldn't be able to fully escape the party until the musicians and attendees retired as well.

When Sophia had first arrived at Radbourne, Prudence had given her first pick of the guest chambers. Upon entering this room, Sophia had instantly fallen in love with the rose-colored room and gold, four-poster bed. For some reason, it felt rebellious to surround herself with a shade she had never been able to wear. But what could she say? There were times when a woman must rebel against something, no matter how silly.

Sophia fingered the simple string of pearls around her neck and stared into the looking glass. The lady's maid she and her mother shared had done a lovely job with her hair, twisting and securing it into an intricate pile of curls on the crown of her head. The maid had even tucked in some fern leaves and white alyssum, which complimented Sophia's emerald gown nicely. Even her eyes looked more green than usual.

*I look as well as I ever can,* Sophia thought. Her nose and cheeks had stopped shedding, and, freckles notwithstanding, her once blotchy coloring had finally evened out.

When the strains of a waltz floated up through the floorboards, she smiled a little. Just for a moment, she allowed herself to wonder what it would feel like to glide around in Hugh's arms, oblivious to the stares of others in the room. Would he dance as well as he rode?

She giggled at the memory of them dancing in the meadow all those years before. Unless he'd learned a thing or two during the past decade, he probably had no idea how to dance. She pictured him stumbling his way across the dance floor while stepping on her slippers.

She would laugh all the while.

*Please come,* she thought, hoping she'd at least get the chance to speak with him tonight. It had only been a few days since she'd last seen him, but it felt like ages. She wanted to tell him that Mrs. Danforth had left with not one, but *two* beloved dogs. As Sophia had waved farewell, she realized that in a few days, when the house party was scheduled to conclude, she would be forced to say goodbye to Hugh as well.

Sophia swallowed against the lump in her throat and straightened her shoulders. Time to go.

She met Prudence coming up the stairs as she was going down. Her sister wore a lovely gown almost the exact shade of pink as the drapes in Sophia's room, and how well it looked on Prudence. Sophia nearly laughed at the unfairness of it.

"Oh, good," her sister said. "I was just coming to hunt you down."

"Preferably not to shoot me, I hope," Sophia quipped.

"No, but I will threaten to do exactly that if you are considering crying off from tonight's festivities."

"Why would I cry off?" Sophia asked. "Honestly, Pru. One would think you have no faith in your sister."

"Oh, I have every faith in you," Prudence insisted. "But I also know you are sad, and when I am sad, I want to crawl into bed and be left alone."

Sophia considered denying it, but there was no fooling her sister. Besides, Sophia *had* been sad. Pitiful, lonely, and sad. But if there was even a chance she would see Hugh tonight, she was not about to hide away in her room. Wallowing would come later, after she had danced and enjoyed a few moments with him.

"I am dressed, I am here, and I am ready to enjoy myself," said Sophia firmly. "Is there anything I can do before the guests arrive?"

"That's the spirit." Prudence slipped her arm through her sister's and pulled her down the few remaining stairs. At the bottom, she stopped and lowered her voice. "Mr. Quinton hasn't sent his regrets, so I assume he is planning to attend, but no one has seen him all day. Have you?"

Sophia's hopes plummeted at the news. How frustrating that one single person could have such control over another. He was still gone?

"You honestly don't know what has kept him so occupied of late, do you?" Prudence asked.

They'd had this discussion before, to which Sophia had said, "If anyone would know about his whereabouts, it would be Knave."

"It would be you." came her sister's reply.

No matter how many times Sophia told Prudence that Hugh did not owe her an explanation, apology, or anything else, Prudence chose to believe otherwise. In her sister's mind, Sophia and Hugh were essentially betrothed, which was certainly not the case.

"I haven't spoken to him since the night of Mr. Fawcett's return," Sophia finally said. She stared worriedly at the front entrance. Where could he be? Had something happened to waylay him? Was he hurt or injured somewhere? Perhaps they should go in search of him.

She was about to express her worries when the large wooden door opened, and the object of her concern slipped inside. Hugh tugged off his gloves and removed his hat, revealing wet hair. Goodness, he was damp from head to toe. He rubbed his hands together, as though chilled, then stiffened when she caught his eye.

"Sophie," he whispered, causing her heart to puddle at her feet. She wanted to rush forward and throw herself into his arms. How she'd missed him. Even in his disheveled state, no one had looked more handsome.

The way they stood there, staring at each other, one would think they were back in the drawing room that first night of the house party, seeing each other after nearly a decade.

*Say you love me too,* she thought fiercely. *Say the gap that distances us doesn't matter to you because it doesn't matter to me.*

Of course he said nothing of the kind. Words such as those were only spoken in her dreams.

He finally cleared his throat and took a step towards her. "You look beautiful, Sophie." He seemed to realize she wasn't alone and quickly added, "As do you, Lady Knave."

Prudence giggled. "I would compliment you in kind, sir, but you appear a trifle unkempt. Do not say you intend to miss the soirée, sir, or I will tell you what I've only just told

Sophia—that I will hunt you down and very possibly shoot you."

He grinned. "Are you a good aim, my lady?"

"Good enough."

"Then I wouldn't dare miss the party."

"Smart man," said Prudence. She studied him a moment before adding, "You have been very busy of late."

He tucked his hands behind his back and shrugged guiltily. "I've had some pressing matters to attend to. You'll have to forgive me."

"Since you have returned in time for the soirée, I forgive you," said Prudence. "Sophia, on the other hand, will likely require some groveling. You have been missed, sir."

After an awkward silence, in which Sophia silently wished her sister to the devil, Prudence cleared her throat. "If you'll both excuse me, I need to speak with the musicians before our guests arrive. Good to see you, Mr. Quinton."

Sophia watched her sister disappear around the corner with a roll of her eyes. What had Prudence been thinking to say such a thing? Honestly.

Not knowing how to undo the damage, Sophia finally shrugged and confessed, "You *have* been missed, Hugh."

An emotion that appeared like longing flared in his eyes before he blinked and looked away.

"Sophie," he said, "there's something I need to speak to you about. I was planning to do it later, but . . . well, I suppose now's as good a time as any."

The pained tone of his voice told her that what he had to say was not something she would want to hear. He seemed to drag his eyes back to hers again, and the moment their gazes locked, she saw the sadness. Like a reflection of her own expression, it stared back at her, raw and unyielding.

*He's going to say goodbye*, she realized with a start.

His increased preoccupation with business matters, his withdrawal from the house party over the past several days, the look on his face now—they were all stepping stones to this point.

*No*, she thought. *You are not going to say goodbye yet, not like this.* Would she not even get her dance?

"Forgive me," she blurted, her voice trembling, "but I'm afraid our conversation will have to wait. I must help Prudence now."

He reached out as if to stop her, but she backed away, shaking her head. "The guests will be arriving any moment, and you are not properly dressed. You'd best hurry."

"Please, Sophie, don't go."

"I will see you later." Tears stung the corners of her eyes, but before they betrayed her, she strode away. Only instead of going to her sister, she rounded the corner and escaped into the dark, empty library. With her back pressed against the door, she focused on filling her lungs with air and keeping the tears from falling.

She had suspected she would have to let him go eventually, but she wasn't prepared to do so just yet. One more day. She only needed one more day to enjoy herself and forget that life didn't always play out as she wished it would.

A traitorous tear slipped down her cheek, and she angrily wiped it away. How dare he set her to crying now, right before the party was about to begin. It was most unfair, especially considering he hadn't appeared nearly as upset.

*Pull yourself together, Sophia.*

She closed her eyes and allowed herself one last deep breath before she straightened, wiped what remained of the dampness from her eyes, and lifted her chin.

She was through making a fool of herself over a man,

and she refused to cower in the library any longer. She would go out, greet their guests with a cheerful disposition, dance, play cards, and laugh with her neighbors and friends.

She would *not* be sad.

# TWENTY-ONE

SOPHIA SPIED HUGH the moment he walked into the ballroom. He'd arrived almost thirty minutes late, looking far too handsome for her peace of mind. Most men wore white cravats and white shirts, but not Hugh. He always matched his neck ties to the color of his coats, as though making a statement to all others in the room. *I am not like you, nor do I wish to be.* Sophia had always liked how he dressed. One more thing that set him apart.

Tonight, he looked like a character from one of her sister's books—tall, dark, and mysterious. With the exception of his white shirt and dark gray waistcoat, he wore all black. Factor in his dark hair and chocolate brown eyes, and Sophia had a difficult time keeping her eyes off of him.

Throughout the first half of the evening, she was able to avoid him completely. Every time he moved in her direction, she would approach the nearest unattached gentleman she knew and engage him in conversation. It was an effective tactic because when the musicians announced a new set, they'd inevitably ask her to dance. Normally, she was only occasionally partnered, but tonight, Sophia danced them all.

She reacquainted herself with the steps of the country

dance, the scotch reel, and the cotillion. She also remembered exactly why she didn't care for dancing. All that prancing about in the center of the room, with onlookers judging her many ineptitudes—no, dancing wasn't for her. Unless, of course, Hugh were to ask her for a waltz.

It was a conundrum, really. She desperately ached for his company while being petrified of it at the same time. At one point during the cotillion, she briefly caught his eye from across the room.

*Don't say goodbye,* she silently pleaded. *Please, don't say goodbye.*

When the dance finished, her partner led her to her sister's side before bowing and taking his leave.

Prudence elbowed Sophia with a grin. "Aren't you popular this evening."

Sophia was busy scanning the room, looking for Hugh. Where had he gone? She was growing weary of the avoidance game and craved his presence more than anything.

"After three London seasons," said Sophia, "I have finally learned how to cajole a man into asking me to dance. I need only engage him in conversation, wait for the dance to begin, and *voilà,* I have a partner."

Prudence chuckled. "Who are you and what have you done with my sister? If I remember correctly, during the last ball we attended in London, you said something along the lines of never wanting to dance again."

Sophia continued to scan the room. "A woman can change her mind."

"Your renewed interest doesn't have anything to do with avoiding a certain man, does it?"

"I don't know what you're talking about." Ah, there he was, speaking with—

Sophia's eyes widened in shock. Was he actually speaking with her mother, and amicably at that? Her mother laughed at something he said and playfully tapped him on the arm with her fan. Sophia could hardly believe it.

She latched on to her sister's arm and nodded in the direction of their mother. "Are you seeing what I am seeing?"

Prudence didn't respond right away, but when she did, there was an element of surprise in her tone as well. "Good for you, Mother," she murmured.

Another country dance was announced, and Hugh looked up, meeting Sophia's gaze almost instantly. She stared at him in wonder as he leaned forward and said something that made her mother smile once more. Then he bowed politely and began walking towards Sophia.

This time, she didn't hunt down the nearest unattached man. She waited with bated breath, trying with all her might not to hope for a different outcome than a farewell.

"Sophia, would you honor me with this dance?" a familiar voice intruded, yanking her out of a beautiful dream that felt so close to becoming a reality.

She blinked and looked at the intruder. "Mr. Fawcett," she stammered. "I—"

"It's Jacob, remember?"

She sighed, accepting her fate. "Forgive me, Jacob. And yes, it would be a pleasure to dance with you."

He bowed and held out his hand. As she took it, she glanced at Hugh once more, just in time to see him change directions and walk away.

She wanted to run after him and make sure he knew she had no interest in Mr. Fawcett or he in her. Didn't Hugh realize that *he* was the object of her affections?

*Oh Hugh,* she thought. *What is it you want?*

"I danced with Catherine." Jacob's voice interrupted her thoughts again as they lined up for the set, and Sophia had to remind herself that he was probably feeling equally distracted and frantic. Only in his case, she had information that could possibly ease his mind, assuming he could be patient.

"How was she?" Sophia asked when the steps of the dance brought them together.

"Seemed her usual, lovely self," was all he could say before they parted company.

*Bravo, Catherine,* Sophia thought. *At least one of us can retain her composure.*

As soon as they joined hands again, Jacob added, "Have you had a chance to speak with her?"

Sophia only had time to nod before they were required to step back into the line again. She thought about how to answer as she waited for other couples to dance in the middle, and as soon as it was her turn again, she spoke quickly.

"I believe she needs some time to adjust to the change in circumstances."

Back to the line they went, waited, then joined hands once more. "I suggest you give her a day or two then ask how she'd feel if you stayed a while longer."

They parted ways again. Good grief. Country dances could be maddening when one was trying to carry on a serious conversation.

As soon as Sophia could speak to him again, she added, "She is in a tender place, having lost a beloved husband, but I think she is open to the idea of getting to know you better."

His smile was the only response she got until they met up in the center of the rows. "I was not wrong to hope?" he asked.

"No."

His smile widened, and when they joined hands again, he added, "Thank you, Sophia."

The musicians played on and the dancers continued to

move through the steps. Jacob carried the conversation, but by that point, Sophia was only half attending. Her thoughts had latched onto his words: *I was not wrong to hope.*

Was *she* wrong to give up on Hugh and always assume life would disappoint her?

Perhaps she needed to take her own advice for once.

As soon as the dance ended, she began searching the room once more. *Hugh, where are you?*

"Sophia," Jacob grabbed hold of her hand, forcing her to look at him. "I haven't had the chance to speak to your mother yet, but I believe she looks a little parched." He winked. "Perhaps I'll procure a glass of punch and take it to her now."

Sophia felt another stab of guilt at what she'd asked him to do. It hadn't been fair, and she shouldn't allow him to go through with it.

She shook her head. "It was wrong of me to ask that of you. Please forget your part of our agreement and take the punch to Catherine instead."

He backed away with a grin and winked again. "I never forget." Then he spun on his heel and headed for the refreshment table.

Sophia could only watch him go while berating herself for being a coward.

She looked over the room once more, searching for Hugh, but he was not to be found. Her sister, on the other hand, stood clinging to her husband's arm and looking radiant. Abby was there too, smiling as Brigston placed a kiss on her temple. Not far away, Catherine had met up with Jacob at the refreshment table and now laughed with him about something.

A weariness settled over Sophia, or perhaps it was a heavy heart. She had wasted so much time avoiding the one person she wanted to be with the most. Even if Hugh planned to tell her goodbye, it would have been better to hear him out. Perhaps she could have convinced him to stay a bit longer. Maybe all he needed was more encouragement.

Had she lost her chance? Had he already gone back to his room?

What a fool she'd been.

The room felt suddenly warm, so she wove her way through the throng of people and stepped onto the balcony, where it was much less crowded. It was growing dark, and the air was still thick with humidity, but the drizzle had finally subsided, leaving behind a refreshing scent.

She breathed in the country air and rested her elbows on the balustrade, wishing she could take Dominicus for a ride.

"Let me guess," a blessedly familiar voice said at her side. "You're aching to go for a ride right now."

Sophia gasped and turned quickly. "Hugh," she breathed, so relieved to see him. "I thought you'd gone. I thought you'd given up on me. I thought—"

He picked up her hand and brought it to his lips. Even through her lace gloves, she could feel his warmth and the power of his touch. It spread through her entire body, easing the weariness and making her feel alive once more.

"I came here tonight to speak with you. Do you truly think I'd retire before I'd accomplished my purpose?"

"No," she said. *It's just my dratted tendency to assume the worst.*

"You're cold." He gave her fingers a squeeze before releasing them to remove his jacket, which he slung over her shoulders.

"Really, there's no need." Even as she said it, she pulled the jacket closer to her, relishing the warmth it offered, along with the scent of sandalwood. If only he was still in it, hugging her from behind the way she'd seen Knave do with Prudence countless times.

"I'm sorry I've been avoiding you," she admitted. "I was certain you intended to say goodbye, and I didn't want to hear it."

He rested his elbows on the stone railing and, with his arm touching hers, looked up into the almost dark sky. "We'll have to say our goodbyes eventually, you know."

"Why?" she quietly asked, because she honestly didn't know.

He smiled sadly. "Because we must, Sophie."

*So that is that,* she thought with a shiver. He was going to leave without a fight, without asking if he could stay a few days more. He didn't even say he'd miss her as well or suggest they meet up in London during the next season.

Her fingers clung to the fabric of his coat as if it would somehow keep him here. She pressed her lips together, wondering if she'd ever feel truly happy again. Before he'd reentered her life, it had been easy to live without him. Now, however, it felt impossible, like he'd be taking a vital part of her with him when he left.

*You'll mend,* she told herself. *You will. It'll take time—probably a lot of time—but one day you will be genuinely happy again. Everything will work out as it should.*

It felt like a lie, but at least she wasn't on the brink of tears. If anything, she felt numb.

"It's beautiful here," he said.

"Yes," she agreed.

"Spending time at Talford, and with you, brought back some good memories."

So that's all she was to him. A pleasant memory that was destined to become a pleasant *distant* memory. How very unfair.

Once upon a time he'd been a good memory too. Now he'd become an excessively painful one.

"I believe you'll do great things with it."

It took her a moment to digest his words. What an odd thing to say. Do great things with what? Talford? How could she possibly when they'd only recently agreed it would have to be sold?

"I'm leaving in the morning," he blurted out the words as though they'd been weighing him down, and it relieved his mind to spew them out.

She swallowed, knowing she should say something. But what? He'd already made up his mind and didn't seem interested in her opinion. Perhaps a joke would ease the pain in her chest.

"It's my freckles, isn't it? Try as you might, you cannot like them."

He snickered and twisted to face her. After watching her a moment, he lifted his hand to trail a finger along her cheek. As he did so, his smile disappeared.

"If only that were the case," he murmured.

"My red hair?" she asked, hoping he'd continue touching her.

He shook his head and let his hand fall back to the railing. "You know that's not it, Sophie."

"If it's because of Mr. Fawcett, I should tell you that he and I are not—"

"He is a good man," Hugh interrupted. "If you give him a chance you could do well together."

"But—"

"You and I are not equals," Hugh said with a grimace, as though it pained him to say it. "We never will be. Marry Mr. Fawcett. Turn Talford around, help as many animals as you'd like, and be happy. Please, Sophie, be happy."

She stared at him as a wrenching pain pierced the protective numbness, driving deep into her soul. Without him she couldn't possibly be happy. It was like asking her to be content with never riding again or feeling the sun on her face or the wind in her hair. Could he not see that he'd become the primary contributor to her happiness?

Perhaps it was wrong to give someone else that much control. But when a person chose to love another, that was the natural consequence. By opening her heart to Hugh, she had given him the power to heal, to love, or to hurt—the power to affect her emotions one way or the other.

The only way to take back that power was to stop loving, stop remembering, and stop caring.

So no, Sophia couldn't be happy. Not yet. Not until Hugh's memory became far more distant and much less painful. If he didn't understand that, then he didn't know what it felt like to love.

Ever so slowly, she removed his coat from her shoulders and laid it on the railing next to him. A burst of cold enveloped her, but that was the least of her worries.

"Goodbye, Hugh," she whispered before walking away.

He didn't call out to her or try to stop her. He didn't say he'd miss her. He didn't even return her goodbye. He just let her go.

That hurt most of all.

As she made her way back through the crowded ballroom, the musicians began playing a waltz.

# TWENTY-TWO

SOPHIA MADE IT halfway up the stairs when her mother caught up with her—or rather, her mother's voice.

"Where are you going?" She did not sound happy.

Sophia stopped and sighed inwardly. Apparently Jacob had followed through on his promise to speak to her mother. It was good of him, truly. But honestly, what rotten timing.

"I'm not feeling well and am going to bed, Mother." She started walking up the stairs again, only to hear her mother's footsteps in pursuit. Tempted to run ahead and bolt the door, Sophia had to force her steps to remain even. Unfortunately, running away was something only a child could get away with.

She continued forward to her bedchamber, then waited for her mother to enter before closing the door.

*You mustn't cry yet,* she told herself, not daring to look her mother in the eye. The vulnerability and pain she felt was probably obvious.

Sophia began removing her gloves, hoping for a quick scold. Perhaps if she went on the offensive again.

"Have you come to tell me that Mr. Fawcett has developed a romantic interest in Catherine instead of me?"

To Sophia's surprise, her mother didn't rant or demand Sophia return to the ballroom. Instead, she sighed and sat down in a chair near the fireplace. "So it's Catherine who has drawn his notice, is it? I should have known."

"They could be very happy together," said Sophia.

Silence. Then a quiet, "What about you, daughter? Is there someone who could make *you* happy?"

*Yes, only he doesn't feel the same and will be leaving on the morrow.*

It was the wrong thing to think, because tears begin to burn in her eyes.

"No," she managed to say with a shaky voice, leaving it at that. She sat on her bed, frantically blinking the tears away, and slowly removed her slippers.

"Mr. Quinton paid your father and me a visit earlier today."

"Did he?" Sophia focused on the floorboards. Her eyes followed the grooves, making a pathway through the planks.

"He located some land not too far from here that could be used to create additional tenant farms. According to his calculations, it would be possible to make Talford self-sustaining again—assuming we use your dowry to purchase the land. He even had a contract drawn up with the seller's signature, giving us until the end of the year to come up with the money." She paused. "He said the idea came from you."

*So that's what Hugh had been up to,* Sophia thought. He hadn't been making himself scarce. He'd been doing yet another thing for her—something that further endeared him to her. No wonder he'd told her to marry Jacob and make something of Talford.

The realization made her feel even more miserable somehow. *How can I make something of Talford now, Hugh? I have no more marriage prospects. All of your efforts were for naught.*

Sophia wasn't sure what her mother expected her to say

or do. Did she want Sophia to go back to the ballroom and fight for Jacob? Place an advertisement in the papers for a potential husband? Or did she simply want Sophia to feel the full weight of her mistakes?

"I am sorry for disappointing you, Mother."

"Oh, my dear, you haven't disappointed me. On the contrary, you've impressed me. I have come to see a new side of you through the eyes of Mr. Quinton. He made it very clear that you ought to have a say in Talford's dealings from here on out. The more I think on it, the more I believe he is right. I'm very much afraid your father and I have underestimated you, and for *that*, I am sorry."

Her words had probably been spoken to make Sophia feel better, but they didn't. None of it mattered anymore.

"Be that as it may, Talford will still have to be sold," Sophia said woodenly.

"Will it?" Something in her mother's voice made Sophia finally look up.

"When your father agreed to sell a small portion of our land to Lord Bradden in exchange for enough funds to pay off our debts and secure your dowry, Lord Bradden knew your father couldn't be trusted with the money. The contract stipulated that the funds would be invested in the exchange, where it would remain until you married. At that point, both his and your father's signatures will be required to release it."

Sophia wasn't aware of the extent Lord Bradden had gone to in order to secure her dowry, but that didn't exactly help her now.

Her confusion must have been apparent because her mother added, "I simply wonder if, given the circumstances, Lord Bradden and your father would be willing to make an adjustment to the contract. Perhaps if you present your and Mr. Quinton's plan for the new tenant farms, Lord Bradden would agree to give the money directly to you instead of your future husband."

Sophia stared at her mother, her mind whirling. "What are you saying, Mother?"

"I'm saying that your dowry has not served its intended purpose and some renegotiations might be in order."

"Contracts can be altered, just like that?"

"If all parties involved agree to the alterations, then yes—at least this particular contract."

"Why has no one ever told me this before?"

"What difference would it have made?" her mother said. "Even if we had given the money directly to you three years ago, what would you have done with it?"

"I . . . don't know."

Her mother sat back in her chair and sighed. "More than anything, your father and I wanted you to marry, Sophia, and having a dowry is a great advantage. If things had worked out differently—if you had agreed to wed during one of your seasons or if Mr. Fawcett had come up to scratch—then. . ."

"Everything would have worked out as planned."

"Yes."

"So why tell me now?" Sophia asked, too overwhelmed to make sense of anything.

"Because circumstances have changed. Because you may never marry. Because Mr. Quinton has found an investment that could be more beneficial to you than the exchange. And because I now believe that you, my dear Sophia, may very well have it in you to make something of Talford again."

Sophia began trembling. Her mother's touching words. Her faith. *Hugh's* faith. His rejection. The gaping hole he'd left in her heart. It was all too much. Her emotions collided, causing the tears to spill down her cheeks.

"What if I can't, Mother? What if I fail like I failed at finding a husband?"

Her mother sat beside her on the bed and wiped the tears from her daughter's cheek. In a soft and gentle voice, she asked, "What if you don't?"

SOPHIA SLEPT FITFULLY, finally giving up when the skies became a murky gray and the glow of the sun hovered just below the horizon. She crawled from her bed to peer through the window. At some point during the night, the clouds had thinned, leaving behind the perfect amount of fluff for a spectacular sunrise. She watched the glow, waiting for the shimmering rays of light to splay through and around the clouds.

Hope. That's what sunrises were. A visual nudge to look for the beauty in the day ahead. And oh, how Sophia wanted that hope to fill her heart like the light would soon fill the skies.

She was tired of sadness.

The sound of carriage wheels scraping against gravel intruded, drawing her gaze to the coach below. Diminutive and a bit rugged, the antithesis of the man who would soon climb inside, the coach sat beneath her like a bad omen, taunting and telling her no hope could be had.

Park exited the house carrying two large bags. Behind him trailed two footmen with a trunk. Hugh and Knave appeared next, talking like old friends. They shook hands, and just like that, Hugh climbed into the carriage.

Pain lurched inside her. She quickly pulled the drapes closed and stepped back, willing herself not to cry. When the tears came regardless, she told herself it was because her lovely sunrise had been spoiled and not because Hugh had gone.

Sophia eyed her warm and comfortable bed with longing, wanting to crawl back under the bed clothes and sleep away the pain. But after the sleepless night she'd had, that wouldn't work. She would only toss and turn and continue to dwell on her sorrows.

No, what she needed most was to keep her mind occupied on something other than Hugh. And she would. She would summon her maid, dress, and pack her belongings. Then she would return to Talford and begin the process of saving her home.

It took two days and a great deal of pleading to convince Lord Bradden and her father to adjust the stipulations in the contract regarding the money set aside for her dowry. Once agreed, it took another fortnight for the paperwork to be readied.

Sophia would never forget the worried look Lord Bradden gave her as he held the quill in his hand, not quite ready to sign.

"Are you certain you wish to do this?" he asked.

She'd replied with a confidence she almost felt. "I am."

"It's a great risk."

"I know."

"If it turns out to be a poor investment—"

"It won't."

He sighed, as though he'd done all he could to steer her away from folly, then scribbled his name at the bottom. Her father followed suit, and Sophia left the room a wealthy woman.

As Lord Bradden had counseled her earlier, the safest thing would be to sell Talford for whatever price they could get, purchase a small cottage somewhere, reinvest the money in the exchange, and live off the interest.

Unfortunately for him, Sophia wasn't interested in playing it safe. She'd done that her entire twenty-two years and only look where it had taken her. Hugh may have walked out of her life, but he'd left her with a plan. A solid plan. She intended to move forward, be bold, and fight for the best life could offer her.

It was a frightening prospect, to be sure, but also thrilling.

Outside, she tilted her face towards the sun. How she loved the country for its open space, earthy scents, and people who, for the most part, accepted her as she was. She was through with London seasons, expectations, and rules that dictated she must wear a hat while out of doors. Bonnets were all well and good at times, but sometimes a woman needed to feel the sun on her face.

The sound of laughter pulled her from her thoughts, and Sophia looked over to see Jacob and Catherine rounding the corner of the house. She tried not to feel envy at their obvious camaraderie, choosing to think instead that Jacob had been right to stay in Lynfield, and Catherine had been right to open her heart to him. They seemed truly happy together. It was a difficult sight to behold, but also beautiful.

"Sophia!" Catherine quickened her stride, meeting up with Sophia at the bottom of the steps.

"It seems like an age since I've last spoken to you. I thought for certain you would come to see Abby and Brigston off last week, but we missed you.

Sophia gave her a rueful smile. "I should have been there, I know, but they came by Talford the evening before to

215

say farewell, and I . . . well, there are only so many goodbyes I can tolerate. Thank goodness you aren't going anywhere."

"Not permanently, but . . ." Catherine slipped her arm through Jacob's and gave him a shy smile. "I may leave for a few weeks. Jacob has invited me to meet his sister and aunt in Surrey, and I am considering it."

"And *I* am trying not to pressure her," added Jacob with a grin.

Sophia tried not to dwell on the fact that it had taken her and Jacob six months to call each other by their Christian names, and he had never once invited her to visit his family.

Hmm . . . yet another sign the pair in front of her were far more suited to each other than she and Jacob had ever been.

"I hear Surrey is lovely this time of year," Sophia said.

"That's what I have been telling her."

"You have also told me about your dramatic and, dare I say, difficult sister."

He laughed. "She is that, but not to worry, my dear, I will shelter you from her extremes."

Sophia tried to keep her surprise to herself. They'd progressed to endearments already, had they? Huh. Was there to be a wedding at Christmas then? Possibly sooner?

"Assuming you agree to accompany me, that is," he added.

"Which I haven't."

"Not yet."

She chuckled and shook her head before turning her attention back to Sophia.

"How are you, Sophia? I hear you have been quite busy of late."

"I am well, thank you. And yes, very busy." As thrilled as Sophia was for the pair, she wasn't ready to be in the company of such obvious affection just yet. Perhaps when the pair returned from Surrey, it would be easier.

"I'm afraid I must be on my way," Sophia said. "I am meeting with our groundskeeper and a few of our tenants and am expected back at Talford. Catherine, if you decide to go with Jacob, do not worry. You will win over his aunt and sister in no time. From the sounds of it, his sister could benefit from the example of a mature and exemplary woman in her life, and who better to provide that than you?"

Catherine responded by giving Sophia a hug. "Good luck with your meeting."

"Safe travels to you," Sophia returned with a smile. She walked to her carriage and allowed the waiting footman to assist her inside.

Under normal circumstances, she would have ridden Dominicus to Radbourne, but she hadn't lied about her meeting. Earlier, she had arranged to collect her grounds-keeper and a few of her more knowledgeable tenants to take them to see the land Hugh had located. Before she signed the purchase agreement, she wanted a few more opinions on the project.

She'd invited her father as well, but he declined, saying it was her money and therefore her decision what to do with it.

Sophia was officially on her own.

# TWENTY-THREE

HUGH SORTED THROUGH the morning's post at the desk in his study, pausing when he came to a letter with a familiar feminine script.

*Sophie.*

He gripped it tightly between his fingers. It had been over two months since he'd left Radbourne, but when he didn't hear from her right away, he didn't expect to hear from her again.

Why had she written? To thank him? Inform him of her recent betrothal and tell him she would soon be purchasing the land he'd found? He couldn't think of any other reason she'd write.

Memory after memory invaded. He could almost smell the scent of lavender she often wore, or perhaps he just wanted to smell it.

Park cleared his throat. "You won't learn what's inside by starin' at it."

"I'm not sure I want to know what's inside."

"So toss it in the fire and always wonder."

Park was never one to mince words. But he was right. Better to know than wonder.

Hugh cracked the seal and unfolded the paper. Several words and sentences had been blotted out, making him smile. Most women would have rewritten it without the blotches, but not Sophie.

She was perfectly imperfect.

*Dear Hugh,*

*I wanted to thank you yet again for all you have done for me and my family.* <several words blotted out> *You accomplished what you set out to do, and I find myself* <another blotch> *deeply in your debt. The land you located seems perfect for its intended purpose. There are some areas that need to be leveled and cleared, and a few ditches to dig, but I have located capable and honest men to do the work. By spring, we hope to have at least five new tenants. There is room for more, I realize, but I thought it best to develop the land in stages.*

*Smart girl,* Hugh thought, even as pain constricted his chest. Apparently, she'd already married, and Mr. Fawcett was now happily ensconced at Talford Hall. The thought made him want to toss the letter into the fire right then, but he forced himself to continue.

*Hugh,* <more blotches> *I couldn't have done any of this without you. I'm still uncertain as to the outcome of the venture—if all will work out as planned—but I am hopeful, which is something I haven't felt in a while.*

*I debated about writing you, as it is frowned upon for* <another blotch> *an unattached woman to write an unattached man, but I can be a bit rebellious at times. I still ride without a bonnet, after all.*

Hugh paused to reread that last paragraph. She was still unattached? How? Her dowry had been needed for the purchase of the land.

He read on greedily, hoping for answers.

> *If Prudence and Knave knew about this latest rebellion—that I am writing you—they would send their hellos.* <more blotches> *As would Catherine and Mr. Fawcett, who have recently become betrothed. They plan to invite you to the wedding and are hopeful you will accept.*
>
> <Two full lines blotted out>
> *In the meantime, please accept my best wishes.*
> <another blot>
> *Sophie*
>
> *P.S. Tell Park hello and that I like the color of his hair.*

Hugh set the letter down as several emotions ran through him. Curiosity. Wonder. Confusion. Relief. Why the latter, he had no idea. It wasn't as though he could race back to Lynfield and ask her to marry him himself. But at least now he wouldn't have to envision her with another man. It was selfish, really, but sometimes a man was selfish.

He leaned back in his chair, steepling his fingers under his chin. Sophie had discovered a way to purchase the land without marrying. Had she found an investor or had she convinced her father that the money for her dowry should go to her rather than her future husband?

Hugh wanted to know. He wanted to know about the men she'd hired to do the work and how she had found them. He wanted to know how the plans were progressing and what changes she'd made. He wanted to know what tenants would one day inhabit the farms and how it would all come to fruition.

He also wanted to know how Catherine had come to be engaged to Mr. Fawcett, how Lord and Lady Knave fared, and if Sophie had developed any more freckles. Had she taken in other animals? Was she now involved in Talford's day-to-day dealings?

Was she happy?

He especially wanted to know what she'd written under all those dark blotches of ink.

Ignoring the rest of the letters piled on his desk, he pulled out a sheet of paper, dipped his quill in the ink, and began writing. It wasn't until he heard a chuckle that he remembered Park still sat across from him.

"Glad you didn't toss it in the fire, eh?" he gloated.

Hugh paused to crumple a blank sheet of paper and throw it at his employee. "For someone who despises conceit in others, you have more than your fair share of it."

Park laughed. "What you call conceit, I call smarts."

"Off with you, braggart," said Hugh.

Park stood and bowed dramatically. "I'll be in the kitchen, helpin' myself to a slice of last night's cake. Let me know when I can be of service again."

Hugh tossed another ball of crumpled paper at him before Park could escape the room. Only after the door had closed did Hugh return to his letter, purposely adding several blotches of his own.

# TWENTY-FOUR

"MISS GIFFORD . . . Miss Sophia Gifford . . . Miss Gifford," her father murmured as he sorted through the morning's post, making a small pile of letters with Sophia's name on them. He finally grunted and tossed them in her direction. "One would think I was dead in my grave and you had become the mistress of Talford."

Sophia picked up the letters and smiled. "No need to sound so testy, Father. You know as well as I that you are happy these letters are addressed to me and not you. You don't wish to deal with business matters any more than Mother does. You'd prefer to fish, hunt, and enjoy your day, so go. I have things well in hand."

A begrudging smile appeared, and he nodded at her. "Yes, you do." Was that a hint of pride she detected in his voice?

It couldn't be easy for him to see his daughter managing the estate better than he ever had, but he still found it within him to be proud of her. Sophia was grateful for that.

Over the past few months, she had taken over nearly everything, coming to him only when she needed his signature. Any questions she had—and there had been a great many—were usually directed at their solicitor, newly hired bailiff, or Lord Bradden.

Her father pushed his chair back and stood. "You will join us for dinner this evening at Radbourne, will you not?"

"If I am finished speaking with our bailiff, then yes. We are to meet at three o'clock."

"See that you are finished. We would like you to join us." He tossed his napkin on the table and strode from the room.

Sophia sighed before turning back to the post and cracking the seal on the first letter.

The moment she saw *Sophie* written at the top in a bold hand, her breath caught in her throat, and her pulse quickened.

*Dear Sophie,*

*I cannot tell you how XXXXX interested I was to receive your letter. Your words filled me with such XXXXX peace, but also confusion. I can't deny that thoughts of XXXXX Talford have entered my mind often since I left, but I must say that I was hoping for more answers than you gave.*

Sophia frowned at the dark spots, annoyed that she couldn't see the words written underneath. Then she remembered the sorry state of her own letter—which she had rushed to send before she could talk herself out of it—and laughed out loud. He'd blotched words out on purpose.

*Oh Hugh, how I've missed you.*

She carried the letter to a cozy chair near the fireplace and curled up with a happy sigh before reading on.

*Tell me how you funded your investment. Never say you experienced a change of heart regarding Lord D and married him instead. If that is the case, I will be forced to return to Lynfield and challenge the blackguard to a duel. It will be the death of me, as I am a dreadful shot, but I will do what must be done.*

*That said, I'm hopeful I am safe, as your letter stated you are still unattached.*

*I really must know how you managed it. Have you taken up thievery? Will I encounter you the next time I am waylaid by a highwayman? (Or should I say highwaywoman?) Are you selling wares on the streets? Have your pianoforte skills improved since we last met and you are now a famous (infamous?) performer?*

Sophia laughed again, thoroughly enjoying his words while missing him dreadfully.

*Actually, if I had to wager a guess, I would say you used your extensive powers of persuasion to convince your father to rewrite the terms of your dowry and give the money directly to you. Am I right? If so, you need not answer this letter. I'm certain you are busy managing the affairs of Talford Hall.*

*But if I am not correct (as I am hopeful will be the case) I would love to hear the latest exploits involving one Miss Sophie Gifford.*

*XXXXXXXXXXXXXXXXXXXXXXXXXXXXXX XXXXXXXXXXXXXXXXXXXXXXXXXXXXXXXXX XXXXXXX.*

*I wish you well, my friend. There is no one more deserving than you.*

*Hugh*

Sophia frowned at the letter, no longer amused.

*You need not answer. I wish you well. My friend?*

Ever and always his blasted friend!

She dropped the letter to her lap and stared at the dying embers in the fireplace. Apparently she had no reason to write him back any longer, however much she might want to. How frustrating. She'd been purposefully elusive, hoping it would result in a reply, which it had. But would it blossom into more exchanges now? No.

All because the wretched man had guessed correctly and said she need not reply.

Why did he have to be so perceptive? Couldn't he have at least feigned ignorance? Perhaps that had been his aim—to kindly dismiss her from his life yet again.

*His friend?*

*I think not,* she thought sourly. At least friends enjoyed communicating with one another.

She very nearly tossed the page into the fire, but stopped herself just in time. This letter was the only tangible thing she had from him, and . . . well, why destroy it when she could torment herself with it for years to come?

Human emotions were perplexing indeed.

Sophia carried her sour mood with her the rest of the day. She rode Dominicus with reckless abandon, snapped at a groom for snapping at a stable boy, and raised her voice at her bailiff when he suggested they replace their aged and long-standing groundskeeper with a younger, more able-bodied man.

It wasn't until Sophia had stepped across the threshold at Radbourne Abbey and heard her sister's laughter echo through the great hall that she realized she had no desire to surround herself with jovial people. Despite her father's insistence that she join them for dinner, Sophia should have kept her irritable mood to herself and stayed at home.

As soon as Prudence spotted Sophia, she clutched her husband's arm in a dramatic fashion. "Knave, who is that lovely creature? Don't tell me. Is that . . . my sister? I don't believe it. I was certain she had expired."

Knave rolled his eyes and gave Sophia an apologetic look.

"Perhaps I *have* expired," Sophia quipped, "and what you see before you is a ghost, come to haunt the lot of you." She glanced around the room, grateful her sister had kept the numbers small this evening. Only her parents, Lord and Lady Bradden, Prudence, and Knave were in the room. Catherine and Jacob had left for Surrey again to collect his aunt and sister. The wedding was only a fortnight away, and once married, the new family would take up residence in Catherine's modest, but comfortable home.

"You are too freckled to be a ghost," said her mother with a shake of her head. "Why you refuse to wear bonnets is beyond me."

"I wear them, Mother. Just not while I'm riding."

"Sophia, how is your project coming along?" Lord Bradden asked, no doubt wanting to save her from additional censure. Bless his soul.

"Good, I think. It has been a week since I have driven out to check on the progress, but when I was there last, the land had been cleared and leveled where needed, and the houses and fencing are in various stages of completion."

"How exciting," he said. "Would you mind if I accompanied you on your next visit? I would very much like to see it all."

"You would be most welcome, my lord. I am hoping to go tomorrow if that is convenient for you."

Sophia tried not to be sad that her father had never asked to do the same, but it was no use. Today was a day for melancholy, it seemed.

Dinner should have been a scrumptious affair, what with the tender pot roast, carrots, and potatoes, but Sophia could only pick at her food. By the time the group retired to the drawing room after supper, she was beyond weary.

Unfortunately, she had driven over with her parents, and they didn't seem anxious to leave.

Sophia sank down on the sofa and watched the flames dance in the fireplace, trying to ignore the laughter and cheerfulness surrounding her. In that moment, the inner fire she'd clung to throughout the day vanished, leaving behind only sadness.

It suddenly felt as though she'd lost Hugh all over again. She wanted nothing more than to curl into a ball and cry.

Prudence sat beside her, leaning her head on her sister's shoulder. "I know that look," she said. "You are missing him, aren't you?"

*I will not cry. I will not cry. I will not cry.* "I'm just tired is all."

"Of course you are. But you're also missing him. Admit it."

"Yes," Sophia whispered, feeling the traitorous tears flood her eyes. *No. Not here, not now.*

She blinked furiously, trying to keep them from falling. It was one thing to cry in front of her sister or even Knave—another in a room full of people. Her sister tensed at her side.

"Sophia, whatever is the matter?" her mother asked as she sat down on a nearby chair.

"Oh, my dear girl," said Lady Bradden. "Has something upset you? Are you ill?"

*Blast, blast, blast.*

Sophia's face burned in embarrassment, and she shook her head. "I'm fine," she blubbered. "Really, I am. I'm just . . . I-I should go."

Prudence gripped Sophia's arm tightly, refusing to let her stand.

"Isn't it obvious?" Prudence snapped. "She is sad. She misses Mr. Quinton." Sophia could practically feel her sister's growing ire.

*Good grief, Pru, must you tell my sorrows to everyone?* How ridiculously dramatic Sophia must appear, like a silly school girl sobbing over unrequited love. She and Jacob's sister would get along famously.

Knave kindly offered her a handkerchief, which she gladly accepted, wiping at her eyes and nose. Without warning, Prudence leapt from her chair and began pacing the room, her hands balling into fists at her sides.

"I don't understand," she said. "Why did Mr. Quinton leave? It was obvious to everyone that he was in love with Sophia and she with him. Why didn't he stay and fight, like Jacob did with Catherine? Why did he give up so easily?"

"Prudence," said her mother harshly. "This isn't the time for one of your rants."

"No, Mother. It's long past time. That man has broken my sister's heart, and I want to know why."

What *Sophia* wanted to do was crawl into a hole and die. After this humiliation, she doubted she'd dare come back as a ghost.

Lord Bradden's strong but quiet voice filled the silence. "He left because he's a man of honor."

Instead of quieting his daughter-in-law, his words made her more irate. "Honor, you say? Is it honorable to crush a person's soul?"

"Must you be so dramatic?" muttered her mother, with her father immediately adding, "Yes, it *was* the honorable thing to do."

Prudence stopped pacing to glare at her father. "You'll have to explain that to me because I don't understand."

Sophia didn't either, but she didn't necessarily want an explanation at this moment. In a more intimate setting, perhaps, with only her mother and father present, but now? Heavens no. She was certain even the butler was privy to their conversation. No one had bothered to close the doors.

Sophia shut her eyes and prayed for a speedy resolution.

"Prudence, only think what Mr. Quinton would be asking of Sophia if he offered for her," said her father. "He'd be asking her to give up the life she'd been born into, her place in society."

"Sophia doesn't care about society," Prudence argued.

"That's beside the point," her father said. "No man of honor would ask that of a woman he cared about. Mr. Quinton did the right thing."

"No," said Prudence. "The right thing would be to care more about *her* happiness than the opinions of others."

"I'm sure that's what he thought he was doing," said Lady Bradden quietly. "Mr. Quinton isn't the sort to wish unhappiness on anyone, least of all Sophia."

"I would have done the same," added Knave.

Silence followed, and Sophia could see the fight leave her sister—or at least some of it. She turned sorrowful eyes on her husband. "Even if you knew I returned your feelings?"

"Yes," he said. "I would never ask you to give up your place for me."

"What if I wanted to give it up?"

"It's not just about you," he explained. "A decision like that would affect your family as well. Even your friends."

"What if my family and friends didn't care either?" Prudence was nothing if not determined.

He pulled her close and wrapped his arms around her. "You may not care, my love, but there are others who might."

She pulled back to look up at him. "You're saying you would have given me up?"

"With the hope of you finding happiness elsewhere, yes," he said.

With his words, something dark and heavy fell over Sophia, snuffing out whatever hope she'd had left. She crumbled, dropping her head into her hands, and began sobbing. They were silent sobs, thank goodness, but she couldn't keep them from racking her body.

Lady Bradden was the first to speak. "I will send for your carriage, my dear," she said, giving Sophia's shoulder a squeeze.

The others said nothing, not even her sister.

As her father led her from the house to the carriage, Sophia had the sinking thought that if Prudence could think of no more arguments to make, perhaps there were no more to be had.

# TWENTY-FIVE

SOPHIA AWOKE WITH a pounding in her head. She thought it was the wee hours of the morning until she glanced at the timepiece on her bedside table. Was it truly ten o'clock already? It couldn't be.

She lifted her head and peered through her partially open drapes, frowning when she spied charcoal colored clouds.

How perfectly wretched.

A knock sounded on her door, and her mother bustled inside with a tea tray.

"Oh, good. You're up," said her mother. "I was worried I'd have to wake you."

Sophia groaned and dropped her aching head back to her pillow.

The tea tray clattered when her mother set it down, and Sophia could hear a cup being filled.

"Sit up and drink this, Sophia. We need to talk."

"Can we not do this later?" Sophia grumbled. "I didn't sleep well, and my head aches like the devil."

"I assumed that would be the case, so I had the house-keeper prepare you her restorative tea. If you will only drink it, you will feel better shortly. And no, we cannot do this later."

Resigned, Sophia pushed herself to a sitting position and accepted the cup from her mother. She sipped it gingerly, knowing from experience how horribly bitter it would taste.

She grimaced as she swallowed then set the cup aside.

Her mother pulled a chair over and took a seat, folding her hands primly in her lap. She got straight to the point.

"I was thinking about something Knave said last evening, and I have arrived at the conclusion that . . . should Mr. Quinton make you an offer of marriage, I would not be wholly opposed to the idea."

Sophia gaped at her mother, wondering if this was a dream. There was no chance her real mother would even think that, much less say it aloud.

But would her head ache this badly in a dream? Perhaps she'd just heard wrong.

"What are you talking about, Mother?" Sophia asked.

Her mother huffed, as though annoyed she had to repeat herself. "I'm saying that if Mr. Quinton were to ask for your hand, your father and I would give our consent."

Sophia blinked and shook her head, wondering what had brought this on.

Then she remembered the previous evening. The tears, the sobs, her dramatic, humiliating display.

Oh dear. Why hadn't *that* been a dream—or rather, a nightmare?

"Mother," Sophia finally said. "It's kind of you to say all of this, but . . . Hugh is never going to make me an offer of marriage."

"Perhaps he has no plans to at present," said her mother, "but circumstances often change."

"Not mine."

"Now, Sophia," said her mother sternly. "These past few

months I have watched you convince Lord Bradden to rewrite the terms of your dowry. I have seen you make hard decisions, hire capable men, and move forward with plans to save our home. If anyone is capable of changing Mr. Quinton's mind, it is you."

Feeling a bit shaken, Sophia took another sip of tea and winced. Oh, that taste.

"I think your faith in me is misplaced," Sophia said. "I have given Hugh multiple opportunities to confess feelings for me, but he has always remained firm in his resolve to keep me at a distance. Prudence sees what she wishes to see, but she is in error. Hugh does not care for me in that way."

"Now you're giving *me* a headache, child." Her mother leaned over to pour herself a cup of tea, which she drank without even the slightest wince.

She set the cup down with a clatter. "Why do you think I made you promise that you'd choose Mr. Fawcett over Mr. Quinton?"

"Because you wanted me to marry Mr. Fawcett?" Sophia guessed.

"No. Because I could tell Mr. Quinton was falling in love with you, and you with him. Honestly, Sophia. The man set aside his bad feelings for your father to come all this way to help you. I never once saw him look your way without admiration and affection, even when you burned your face and appeared so . . . well, ghastly. Forgive me for saying that, but it's true. He listened to you, valued your opinions, and even convinced your father to do the same. He went out of his way to find a solution to our problems and willingly stepped aside so you could marry someone of your own station."

"Don't be so daft, daughter. Mr. Quinton loves you the way a man *should* love a woman. Of that much I'm certain."

Sophia's mouth fell open. Could it possibly be true? Never before had she wanted to believe her mother as much as she did in that moment.

Overcome with love for the prideful woman at her side—a woman willing to subject herself to society's harsh gossip so her daughter could be happy—Sophia scooted from her bed and threw her arms around her mother.

Once again, tears filled her eyes, only this time, they were hopeful, happy tears.

"He is a good man, Sophia," said her mother with a gentle pat to her back. "I believe you will find much happiness with him."

Sophia pulled away and sat on the edge of her bed, watching her mother. She knew this decision would affect her parents almost as much as it affected her.

"What about you and father?"

With a sigh, her mother smoothed out a few creases in her yellow muslin gown. "I have come to realize that I have been searching for happiness in the wrong places. And your father—well, he'll likely take a little more time to admit he was in the wrong all those years ago, but I believe he'll come around eventually."

She paused and smiled at Sophia. "It's a good thing our daughters are wiser than us. How is your head now?"

"Better."

"Good. Now get dressed and come downstairs. You have a persuasive letter to write."

With those parting words, her mother picked up the tea tray and swept from the room.

Feeling suddenly giddy, Sophia strode to her window and threw her drapes wide. Although the charcoal clouds still coated the skies, she paid them no heed. For her, the sun had come out and made her world bright.

"Thank you, Mother," she whispered. "Thank you."

# TWENTY-SIX

SOPHIA CLUTCHED THE roll of foolscap in her hand as the coach bounced her, Prudence, and Knave down the cobblestone streets. Tense and anxious, she peered out the small window at a less familiar part of London. So this was Lambeth—the place Hugh called home. It was rather nice, actually. Large trees, with only a smattering of orange, red, and yellow leaves left on their branches stood between modest, red-bricked townhouses. The fallen leaves lay scattered on the streets and pathways in a charming display.

Sophia had never been to London in the fall. It seemed less busy, and she liked the sound of crunching leaves as the carriage wheels rolled over top.

When they lurched to a stop in front of a certain townhouse, and Knave announced, "This is it," whatever peace Sophia felt was pushed away as a myriad of butterflies took up residence in her stomach.

Her sister grinned and leaned forward excitedly. "Are you ready?"

From the moment Sophia had enlisted her sister's help with this scheme, Prudence had been bouncing around like a newborn puppy. She'd even begun writing a story about a defiant woman who dared to make an offer of marriage to a man.

Which was precisely what Sophia had come to do—make Hugh an offer he couldn't refuse.

Now, however, as she stared at the white painted door before her, she wondered at her sanity.

"I can't do this," she said under her breath.

"Of course you can, and you will," said Prudence. "This is why you brought us with you—because you knew you wouldn't go through with it without me here to prod you along."

"Shove, more like," said Sophia dryly. She looked past her sister to her brother-in-law and asked, "Am I mad, Knave? Mother thinks I am. She thought a letter would suffice, but I didn't want to write a letter. I need to see his face and know he wants this as much as I do."

Knave shrugged and smiled a little. "You *are* mad, but in a good way. Now go. Tell Park that Mr. Kimball has arrived for his appointment and see how he reacts. We will wait for you here."

The door opened, and the coachman stepped aside.

Sophia inhaled deeply and allowed him to assist her down the step. She looked back only once before squaring her shoulders and clutching the roll of paper she held in one hand and her reticule in another.

At the door, she lifted the knocker and brought it down hard against the wood with a confidence she didn't feel. Then she waited nervously for Park to appear. The door flew open, and his tall, lanky frame filled the opening. He began to say something, only to stop short and gape at her.

"Miss Gifford?" he asked. "What are you doin' 'ere?"

"That's Miss G to you," she said, knowing the man's dislike of lengthy titles or names. "Would you be so kind as to tell Mr. Quinton that Mr. Kimball has arrived?"

A cheeky grin appeared, and Park folded his arms. "You don't look like much of a mister to me, Miss G."

"Glad to hear it." She shuffled her feet nervously. "Are you going to invite me in or shall we continue making a scene? People are beginning to stare."

Park immediately stepped aside and let her in, closing the door behind her. "Am I glad to see you, Miss," he said. "Mr. Q's been watchin' the post and gettin' more temperamental by the day. I'd about made up my mind to write you myself."

His words brought her a much-needed measure of hope, and she nearly hugged him.

"I wish you had," she said instead. "That is a letter I would very much like to read."

He led the way past a small parlor, a set of beautiful mahogany-stained stairs, and a pair of closed doors, before finally stopping in front of a single wooden door at the end of the hall. Park rapped on it once before pushing it open and waving her inside.

She frowned at him and whispered, "Shouldn't you announce me?"

"Right," he said, poking his head inside. "Miss G's 'ere to see you, sir, only now she's wantin' to be called Mr. Kimball."

Sophia returned Park's cheeky grin with a glare. "Very funny," she whispered before forcing her feet to carry her into the room.

Hugh stood slowly, staring at her, perhaps even drinking her in. Or maybe she only thought that because that's what she was doing to him. He appeared slightly older, somehow. There was a new crease on his forehead, and his eyes looked tired and a bit red, as though he hadn't slept in a while.

"Sophie?" he asked, not bothering to hide his astonishment. He stepped around his desk and moved as

239

though he intended to embrace her, only to think twice about it.

He stopped before her and asked, "What are you doing in London?"

*I can do this. I can do this. I can do this.*

She cleared her throat. "I'm here for our meeting, Mr. Quinton. Mr. Kimball, our new bailiff, had other things to attend to this morning, so I've come in his place."

During the past few months, Sophia had come to realize that she was a natural businesswoman. Balancing responsibilities, dealing with servants and workers, and making decisions had come so easy to her, like racing her horse across a meadow. When she'd decided to come to London, she knew that if she could push aside her personal feelings and approach Hugh as she would her solicitor, she might be able to say what she'd come to say.

Hugh shook his head slowly as though trying to make sense of her words. "I'm not sure I understand. Your bailiff wishes to meet with me?"

"Actually, no. Not exactly. I only borrowed his name so I could be sure I'd find you at home this morning. Honestly, Hugh. Do I really have to explain? I came here to see you."

"Why?"

She bit her lip nervously and looked pointedly at the chair situated in front of his desk. "I wish to discuss a business opportunity with you. May I sit down, or do you always keep your guests standing?" Her knees felt ready to buckle at any moment.

"My apologies." He blinked and stepped aside, gesturing to the chair. "I'm just surprised. You're the last person I expected to see this morning. Don't misunderstand, I'm thrilled you've come, but . . . what is this opportunity you wish to speak to me about?"

She sat down, dropped her reticule on the desk, and clamped her fingers around the roll of paper she carried.

Instead of returning to his seat, as she'd expected him to do, Hugh perched his handsome body on the edge of the desk, folding his arms as he looked down at her.

*I can do this,* she told herself yet again. If he rejected her, so be it. He had done it before, and she'd managed to survive.

"I have a proposal for you," she said, frantically trying to remember the speech she'd prepared. It had been perfect. Witty and clever and . . . oh, it was no use. Her mind was a blank.

"I am looking for a man to fill a certain . . . position," she finally blurted. "I think you would be the perfect fit."

Sophia didn't think it possible for him to look more confused, but he did. "I already have a position, so to speak."

"I understand that, and I have no intention of asking you to walk away from your other responsibilities. I simply wish to give you one more."

His eyebrows lifted. "One more responsibility?"

"Er . . . yes."

"What if I don't want another responsibility?" he asked.

She swallowed, thinking that may very well be the case. "Are you not even curious as to what the position entails? If there is one thing I have learned, it's that you shouldn't make a decision without knowing all the facts."

His lips twitched, and he shifted a little, as though making himself comfortable for a good show. "Very well. Tell me more."

*In for a penny, in for a pound,* she thought, trying her utmost to keep her voice steady.

She straightened, lifted her chin, and forced the words out. "I would like to offer you the position of my husband."

She had prepared a long list of reasons why it would be mutually beneficial for them to marry, but all of them evaded her at the look of astonishment on his face.

He stared at her, his eyes wide and his mouth parted.

Sophia suddenly wanted to sink into her chair. She shouldn't have come. She shouldn't have let her mother convince her that Hugh really did love her. And she should never have brought Knave and Prudence along. If they hadn't been there to push her into this, she wouldn't be sitting here now.

This was not a story that Prudence could write the ending as she pleased. This was a real situation with real people, and right now, reality was telling her that she had made a big mistake.

"I'm sorry," Hugh finally stammered. "Did you just offer me the position of . . . your husband?"

Sophia had two choices. She could dash from the room and hope she never saw Hugh again, or she could set aside her fears and see this through. Even if it meant further humiliation, at least she couldn't be called a coward.

Unable to sit any longer, she stood and handed him the roll of paper she carried. "This is an official offer signed by my mother, my father, and . . . me." It sounded ridiculous now that she was saying it out loud, but she forged on nonetheless. "I would like for you to return to Talford Hall as my husband and partner. I understand your own business will take you away from time to time, but I feel up to the task of carrying on without you. I also . . ."

Gracious, this wasn't going well at all. She sounded too stiff and formal, as though this really was a business arrangement. But Hugh wasn't a business arrangement to her. He was . . . Hugh. *Her* Hugh. She needed to put an end to this charade and tell him the truth.

She turned to face him, her body trembling. "I love you, Hugh," she blurted. "I think I always have. I was miserable when I had to say goodbye to you over a decade ago, and I have been miserable since you left last August. A life without you in it is not a life I want."

When he continued to stare at her, she began wringing her hands and pacing again. "If you don't feel the same, feel free to crush my heart into a thousand pieces. But if you do feel, even an inkling—

He took hold of her arm from behind, spun her around, and kissed her.

The smell of sandalwood invaded her senses, and after her initial shock, Sophie melted against him. His mouth was warm and hungry, and he tasted of cinnamon and apples. Sensation after sensation rippled through her body like a caress. Wonder. Hope. Joy. Disbelief.

Kissing him felt even better than she had imagined. She wound her arms around his waist and clung to him, sure she'd fallen out of reality and into a dream.

*Say it'll never end,* she thought.

"What am I to do with you?" he murmured against her lips. She could barely hear him through the happy fog in her brain.

"Marry me," she said.

He drew back and looked down at her, slowly running his hands up her arms to cradle her face. "How I adore you, Sophie."

She smiled up at him before cocking her head to the side. "I was actually hoping for love, but I suppose adoration will do."

He chuckled and kissed her again. "Adoration and love are synonymous in my book."

"Hmm . . . I really don't think that is true," she said with a slow shake of her head. "I've heard you say that you adore chocolate cake before, and I'd like to hope you care for me a little more than that."

He threw back his head and laughed before shaking his head. "If you must know, I adore *and* love chocolate cake, but not nearly as much as I adore and love *you*, Miss Sophie Gifford."

Oh, my. He'd said it. He'd finally said it. He loved her. Hugh, her childhood friend and now her grown up friend, loved *her*. A joy like sunshine on a breezy summer's day wrapped around her.

*I was not wrong to hope,* she thought.

"So you'll accept the position of my husband then?" she asked breathlessly.

He pulled her into a hug and rested his chin on top of her head. "How much does it pay?"

She tilted her face up to him and grinned. "Absolutely nothing."

He frowned. "That will never do. What about . . . oh, I don't know . . . twenty kisses a day?"

She pursed her lips before countering. "Five."

"Fifteen."

"Ten."

"Thirteen, and you have yourself a husband."

She fought her twitching lips before giving in to the happiest of smiles. "You drive a hard bargain, sir. Thirteen it is."

"I believe I shall begin collecting those kisses now." His eyes danced merrily as he tried to kiss her again, but she quickly ducked out of his arms.

"You are not my husband yet, sir. As my betrothed, you are only allotted two kisses a day, which you've already had."

Another frown. "That won't do either. Perhaps we should locate a parson and procure a special license."

"Already done." Sophia lifted her reticule from the desk and gave it a tap. "I have it right here. The parson can marry us as early as tomorrow morning—but only if you are in agreement, of course." She perched on the edge of his desk and waited nervously for his reaction.

He began to chuckle, only to let it die off when she did not join in. "Are you serious?"

"Catherine and Jacob are to be married in nine days. I intend to beat them to it."

He continued to stare at her. "You *are* serious."

"I am."

He slowly walked over to her and reached for one hand, then the other. Delightful shivers traveled up her arms as he trailed his thumbs across her palms.

"As much as I would love to marry you this very moment, Sophie, are you certain that is what you want? Wouldn't you prefer the sort of wedding suited to someone in your station, surrounded by your family and friends?"

Sophia hesitated in her answer. He probably thought she was behaving rashly and would come to regret her impulsiveness, but that wasn't true. She had given this a great deal of thought and had never been more certain of anything.

"I only care that you are there," she said at last. "I have never liked being the center of attention. The mere thought of saying our vows in a room filled with people unnerves me, and that is not how I want to feel on our wedding day. I'd prefer a small wedding."

"Prudence will never forgive you," he said.

"I know," Sophia admitted. "Which is why she and Knave came with me to London. They're waiting in the carriage as we speak."

She threaded her fingers through his and searched his

face. "But that's what *I* want, Hugh. If you'd prefer a big wedding, I'd be happy to oblige. Just know you'll only get two kisses a day until then."

He chuckled softly and sighed. "Big wedding or small, it doesn't matter to me. But, Sophie, what about your mother and father? Do they know you are here? Did they truly sign whatever document it is you brought with you?"

"Yes and yes. Mother thinks I've lost all sense, of course. She thinks I should have written and waited for you to come to me instead. But she wishes us well. She even gave me the gown she wore for her wedding and helped me to alter it. And Father—well, let's just say he's resigned to calling you his son-in-law."

"Our fathers hate each other," he said.

"That is something I intend to change. My father is beginning to see he acted rashly years ago. Give him time."

He pulled her up from the desk and into his arms. "Can we invite Park?"

"Certainly."

"And my father?" he asked. "He is only a fifteen-minute carriage ride from here, and—"

"I would love nothing more," she said. "Should we go there now? Do you think he'll remember me?"

"How could anyone forget you, Sophie?" Hugh trailed his fingers across her cheek and stared into her eyes. "Are you sure about all of this? Are you sure about me? I'm a tradesman and will always be a tradesman. Your life won't ever be the same."

"I'm counting on it."

He finally let out a breath he must have been holding, smiled, and kissed her a third time. She let him because he'd been so agreeable and—well, she rather liked kissing him. When his mouth moved to her neck, she sighed and tilted her head towards his warmth. His lips eventually found hers again, and he combed his fingers through her hair, pulling it free from some of the pins. Sophia clung to him, wanting it to go on and on.

It was probably a good thing they were to marry on the morrow. As he'd said, two kisses a day would never do. Thirteen may not either—not when he made her world so blissfully tipsy.

When he at last released her, she wrapped her arms around his waist and rested her head against his chest, not quite ready to stand on her own.

He kissed the top of her head and murmured. "Did you say Lord and Lady Knave are waiting?"

Sophia's eyes popped open, and she immediately stepped back. Oh, dear. She'd nearly forgotten about her sister and Knave. Prudence was probably ready to charge through the front door and demand to know what had transpired.

"We should probably go," said Sophia, tugging him from the room.

On their way out, they shared the good news with Park, then again with Prudence and Knave in the carriage, and one last time with Hugh's father.

By mid afternoon the following day, Sophia had officially filled the position of Husband, and Hugh received his promised thirteen kisses. Plus a few more.

# EPILOGUE

WEDDING BELLS CHIMED loudly as Catherine and Jacob exited the small stone church located ten kilometers south of Talford Hall. Not a single cloud marred the bright blue sky, but a lovely autumn breeze scattered a colorful array of leaves across the pathway in front of them.

Everyone cheered and tossed handfuls of rice at the couple as they passed. Catherine paused to hug Abby and Brigston, who had arrived two days earlier for the joyful event. Abby's belly now protruded with a nice little bump, but she hadn't let that keep her away.

"I wouldn't have let it keep me from your wedding either, had I been invited," she had told Sophia crossly not long after she arrived.

"You will forgive me once you realize how happy I am," Sophia had replied.

Abby grudgingly smiled and hugged her friend. "You are happy, aren't you? I'm so very glad. I suppose you can make it up to me by christening your first daughter after me."

"Done," said Sophia.

Sophia smiled at the memory, tossing a handful of rice at Jacob and Catherine as they approached. Then she stepped forward to embrace her friend.

"You look radiant," said Sophia. Catherine wore a simple gown of ivory lace with a dusty blue sash tied around her waist. A matching ribbon adorned her bonnet.

"Thank you for bringing him to me," said Catherine. She, too, had been upset when she'd learned of the elopement, but in her current state of bliss, she hadn't taken long to forgive.

The group clustered around the barouche that had been decorated with garlands made of freshly fallen leaves. They waved a hearty farewell to the newlyweds and cheered as the carriage sped off.

Sophia clasped her husband's hand and, when he wrapped an arm around her, snuggled close.

"Do you regret not getting married here?" he asked.

"Not in the least," she said. "We would have had to wait much too long, and have I told you how much I adore being called Mrs. Quinton?"

"Adore or love?"

"According to you, they are one and the same."

He chuckled. "Indeed they are, my adore."

She playfully slapped his chest. "Must you keep saying that? It sounds ridiculous."

"Indeed I must. In the official offer letter regarding my position as your husband, it states clearly that one of my responsibilities is to try your patience daily."

She craned her head to look up at him. "You're wrong. I don't remember writing anything of the sort."

"Because you didn't. It was in my addendum."

"You can't add an addendum, especially not without my signature."

"I can, and I did. Someday, I will show it to you as it contains many important details that you neglected to list."

"What sort of details?"

He pulled her close and dropped a kiss on her forehead. "All in good time, my adore. All in good time."

She frowned, ready to demand a copy of this so-called addendum, when Knave's voice carried across the yard.

"If you could all gather around for a moment, my wife has an announcement."

Sophia slipped her arm through Hugh's and turned a questioning look on her sister. Prudence practically glowed, and her entire body trembled, as though ready to burst.

"I am to be a mother," she blurted. "Can you believe it?"

Knave quickly draped his arm around her and pulled her against his side. "Lest anyone wonder, I am to be a father as well."

Stunned silence met their announcement, followed by cheers and squeals, Sophia's the loudest of them all. She rushed forward and threw her arms around her sister. Abby and their mother raced forward as well, joining in.

"Oh, Pru," Abby said. "This is all too wonderful. How long have you known?"

"For a month, at least. I've been dying to tell everyone, but I didn't want to steal the limelight from Sophia or Catherine. Now that they are both officially married, however, I couldn't wait a moment longer."

"I am so happy for you," Sophia said. "What changed?"

Prudence shrugged. "Nothing, really. I simply took your advice and stopped fretting about it, believing, as you said, that everything would come about as it should. And well . . . it has, hasn't it? For all of us. You, Abby, Catherine, *and* me. It just took a little time is all."

Her sister had never been more right. Everything *had* come about as it should.

"Who knew I could be so wise?" Sophia teased.

Hugh wrapped his arms around her from behind,

hugging her close. "We're all aware of your great wisdom, my love. You did propose marriage to me, after all."

Everyone laughed, including Sophia's parents, both of whom seemed overjoyed at the prospect of becoming grandparents.

"Come," Sophia's father called out jovially. "Mr. and Mrs. Fawcett may have taken the long route back to Radbourne, but if we don't leave soon, they will beat us to their own wedding breakfast, and we can't have that."

Sophia didn't immediately surge forward as the others did. She lingered, hugging her husband's arms to her waist, as she watched her family and friends climb into their various carriages. It had taken three trying seasons, a bucket full of tears, boldness and bravery, but Sophia's dreams of marrying a man she loved had finally come to fruition.

Looking back, it *had* been a journey worth taking. Yes, the setbacks had been wearisome, even heartbreaking at times, but the things she'd learned, the relationships she'd strengthened, and the person she'd become had made it all worth it.

She wasn't naive to think her life would now be free from complications, but if she could hold onto the belief that everything happened for a reason, and all would be well in the end, whatever storms lay ahead could be weathered. She was certain of it.

For now, however, there wasn't a cloud in the sky.

As the first carriage pulled from the yard, Hugh leaned down and kissed her temple, "Shall we be off, my adore?"

"Indeed."

Dear Reader,

Thanks so much for reading! I hope this story gave you a break from the daily grind and uplifted you in some way.

If you're interested in being notified of new releases, or want to check out my other books, you can find me online at RachaelReneeAnderson.com. Rest assured, my newsletter is only sent out when I have a new release (or perhaps a really great sale).

Also, if you can spare a few minutes, I'd be incredibly grateful for a review from you on Goodreads or Amazon. They make a huge difference in every aspect of publishing, and I am always so thankful whenever readers like you take a few minutes to review a book.

Thanks again for your support and best wishes!

*Rachael*

# ACKNOWLEDGEMENTS

This book would have many errors, inconsistencies, and whatnot without the help of some fabulous people.

Alison Blackburn, you are awesome! Thanks so much for always being willing to talk through possible plot ideas and for giving invaluable feedback on the finished draft. You make my writing better, and I am so grateful for your friendship.

Andrea Pearson, bless you for taking time out of your super hectic schedule to beta read for me. Your comments never fail to make me laugh, and I'm so appreciative for all your suggestions and edits.

Karey White, you are the best proofreader there is. Thanks a million for being my friend and finding the time to check over the final draft for me. Fingers crossed I get to read another book from you at some future point.

Karen Porter, you rock. I have no idea how you spot all those little things you but I'm grateful for your gift and feel so blessed to know you.

Kathy with IAmAReader.com and CleanWholesome-Romance.com, What would I do without you? You have helped me with every single one of my books and have been an answer to prayers. I will always be indebted to you.

Jeff, a hundred million thanks for being the husband, father, supporter, confidant, and friend that you are. I love you.

Lastly, I must thank my Heavenly Father. I have very strong beliefs that have taught me who I am, where I come from, and the direction I want to go. That knowledge and inspiration has helped me with each and every one of my stories.

## ABOUT RACHAEL ANDERSON

RACHAEL ANDERSON is a *USA Today* bestselling author and mother of four crazy and awesome kids. Over the years she's gotten pretty good at breaking up fights or at least sending guilty parties to their rooms. She can't sing, doesn't dance, and despises tragedies, but she recently figured out how yeast works and can now make homemade bread, which she is really good at eating. You can read more about her and her books online at RachaelReneeAnderson.com.

CPSIA information can be obtained
at www.ICGtesting.com
Printed in the USA
BVHW042233230320
575809BV00009B/396

9 781941 363263